"A cliff-hanger at the end makes me hope for a sequel ... I felt like Randolph could be a friend, and look forward to meeting him again." —*Deadly Pleasures*

"A refreshingly intelligent story told from the perspective of a dog ... an entertaining who-done-it ... Cozy mystery fans will enjoy this unique, well-written tale."

—FreshFiction.com

"How refreshing that J. F. Englert gives a dog a mystery bone of his own.... [Randolph is] a canine Sherlock Holmes." —fetchdog.com

"I do believe I'm in love.... Randolph is witty, a product of his eclectic reading habits." —*The Jersey Journal*

"A clever premise of using an intelligent dog to be the narrator in this story ... It's very interesting to see the world through a dog's eyes and senses."

—reviewingtheevidence.com

"The fun is in suspending disbelief and looking at the world through the eyes of a dog.... And there's a certain joy to hear from a dog about the rules of 'doing one's numbers' in a public park. If you like that kind of whimsicality and you're a dog person, you'll enjoy *A Dog About Town*." —bookgasm.com

"A hilarious, witty, and touching mystery that reveals both the inner lives of dogs and of New York City ... The plot is tight, and most readers won't see the ending miles away. This is a book that will satisfy dog lovers and mystery hounds alike." —LibraryGoddesses.com

A
DOG
AT SEA

A Bull Moose Dog Run Mystery

J. F. ENGLERT

DELL BOOKS

This is a work of fiction. Names, characters, places, and incidents either
are the product of the author's imagination or are used fictitiously. Any
resemblance to actual persons, living or dead,
events, or locales is entirely coincidental.

A Dell Mass Market Original

Copyright © 2009 by J. F. Englert

Published in the United States by Dell, an imprint of The Random
House Publishing Group, a division of Random House, Inc., New York.

DELL is a registered trademark of Random House, Inc.,
and the colophon is a trademark of Random House, Inc.

ISBN: 978-0-440-24541-4

Cover design: Beverly Leung
Cover illustration: Dan Craig

Printed in the United States of America

www.bantamdell.com

2 4 6 8 9 7 5 3 1

For Penelope

Acknowledgments

I would like to thank Danielle Perez for her fine editorial counsel, everyone at Bantam Dell for their work, Laura Jorstad for her copyediting, Susan Stava for her photography, Posey and the Pollards, Charlie, Ritchie, and Cha Cha, Partners & Crime Bookstore for embracing Randolph, and Claudia Cross and Marcy Posner at Sterling Lord Literistic.

If a dog will not come to you after having looked you in the face, you should go home and examine your conscience.

—Woodrow Wilson

A
DOG
AT SEA

TWO WEEKS AFTER BEING plucked from the lethal waters of New York Harbor by a police helicopter, Yours Truly, a Labrador retriever with a penchant for literature, and Harry, his dangerously abstract and artistic owner, were once again aboard a nautical vessel off our beloved isle of Manhattan. This time, though, the circumstances were quite different.

On our last disastrous waterborne outing there had been nothing but hardship and grimness. There had been nothing delicious to eat. Nothing at all—not even a stale New York pretzel or something seductively sticky and grizzly seared by the sun and a thousand commuters' feet to the steel deck.

Harry and I had chased Imogen, my mistress and his lady love, off the rain-slicked Staten Island Ferry and into the water in the middle of night. Even for a water dog such as myself, this had been harrowing and unpleasant. The conclusion was also ambiguous.

That is, the world was supposed to believe that

Imogen was a victim of those waters never to be heard from again—but Harry and I had a different understanding. We were confident that she had feigned her death and now wanted us to find her in a distant place of her choosing, safe from a world of diplomat-spies, nation-states, profiteers, and other rogues intent on claiming her uranium fortune.

She had left a "constellation map" to lead us to her. This is why we were heading south toward the Caribbean aboard the *Nordic Bliss,* a monstrously oversized, but tidy, Scandinavian cruise ship. In a handful of days' time we would be disembarking on that quaint Dutch island of Curaçao where the architecture is pleasant pastel, the temperature a steady eighty-five degrees. We believed our mistress was hiding there in some cove beneath the stars waiting for us.

As far as our pursuit of Imogen went, passage on the *Nordic Bliss* made sense since it was a "pet lovers' cruise" and something that even scrutinizing and hostile eyes might dismiss as natural for an artist and his dog.

But soon it would become clear that our trip by sea had the trappings of one of those expeditions that start with celebration only to grow progressively more troubled before ending with all hands going down in the middle of the Bermuda Triangle far from hearth and home, gone without a trace. I would learn that the *Nordic Bliss* was chock-full of characters who would threaten to turn this middle-aged Labrador's chin completely white, leading to more than a few encounters

with the absurd and the ridiculous and, most unfortunately, to some untimely passenger deaths. This last
wrinkle would demand the particular abilities of Yours
Truly's 2.3 pounds of smoothly functioning gelatinous
gray matter.

Though doubt and chaos loomed, in these first
shipboard hours the hard edges of recent memory had
gentled somehow, and Yours Truly was able to entertain
a dream of peace—in this case the hope of an eventual
reunion with our Imogen under more permanent circumstances that would eventually leave us all hearthside
again in our cozy Manhattan abode. In the meantime I
harbored the fantasy that I might soon be lazing beneath the shade of Harry's deck chair discreetly dipping into the classics as our drumming liner slid toward
the tropics.

The late-spring sun poured golden light down on
Brooklyn and Staten Island, making even those lesser
boroughs with their factories and sagging docks seem
luminous. Harry tossed a last streamer into the breeze
and watched it sag and flutter down the side of the ship
until it was lost in our wake. There was music playing on
deck—a trio producing Caribbean confections on the
steel drums. Colorful, umbrella-crowned drinks were
being consumed—Harry was draining his perilous third
mojito and swaying a little too loosely for my taste, unable to resist, apparently, the rhythm of the drums and
the ship's wayward risings and fallings. (I sometimes

wonder about my Harry and his endless capacity for distraction.)

There was a team of crew members whose sole responsibility was to smile and distribute bite-sized hors d'oeuvres on paper napkins in our vicinity. These people were such experts, so unflappable and focused in the art of hors d'oeuvres delivery, that even two dozen canines tangled about their feet fervently maneuvering for spillage could not coax a single morsel to the deck.

Though the hors d'oeuvres were whizzing well above this dog's eye level on silver platters overhead, my nose quickly allowed me to develop a tentative list of the unseen delectables. There were in no particular order: urchinmeat salad in endive spears; pepper-crusted goat on brined chestnut with lychee crème fraîche; sea snake with prosciutto, stuffed with muscatelle grapes, wrapped in bacon with a plum reduction; wild snails on crostini; and beef tenderloins on parsnip crisps.

Yes, indeed, a dog's nose—one hundred thousand times more powerful than a human's—is a wondrous tool. (Please remember this the next time you scold your pet for seeming absentminded. Though my brethren do not have my laser-guided brain, reverence for reason, and knack for quiet reflection, they are just as likely to be lost in an ecstasy of scent classification. Expecting them to stay on the rails when rich smells fill the air is the equivalent of expecting a human obsessive-compulsive to take detailed notes during an acid trip.)

But it wasn't these hors d'oeuvres that gave me pause. Certainly had any one of them fallen within easy scooping distance, I would have indulged, but my nose detected even more seductive fare.

I may come across as a bit of a snob for my love of literature, the formality in my writing, or a certain elite bearing with which I carry my plumpish Labrador torso, but I am not a snob. In fact, I detest snobbery.

I have my standards, but for someone who is forced to do his business in public on the streets of New York, be dragged around on a leash, and succumb more often than is comfortable to the lower canine nature, there is a limit to what standards I can have. Also, as a dog I know of the simple, inexpressible joys of existence—and that to pursue these joys you cannot be too proud or you will most surely miss them.

And one of those joys—a joy that was not to be missed—floated somewhere above my head on one of those silver platters. My nose was tormented not by sophisticated endive spears or lychee crème fraîche, but by something common, the gutter child of hors d'oeuvres that makes a mandatory appearance at every wedding, anniversary, and wake in the United States: I am of course speaking of that preservative-laden sublimity *pigs in a blanket*.

A particularly dapper crew member, all blond hair and polished epaulettes, had arrived on deck with a mother lode of these porcine delectables in their individually toasted blankets.

At first, this guardian of the *pigs in a blanket* remained on the fringes of the crowd. All the four-footed animals—even those rare ones unmoved by the other food—instantly became aware of the nearby bounty. The crew member sensed the pack movement in his direction and looked ready to retreat, but then a two-footed animal—a used car salesman from Pasadena, California—gestured for him to approach. The crew member obeyed, gripping the platter against the waves of pointers, hounds, poodles, retrievers, and a single affenpinscher wearing a pink collar.

I am not proud of what happened next and have no excuse for my behavior other than to say that in some cases not to act on our impulses can also be a kind of failure.

The steel drums played on, the Hawaiian-shirted passengers swayed above my head, the *pigs in a blanket* drew closer and closer until there they were right above me. I had not hunted them down, I had only willed them to come in my direction and they had obeyed. This was what they meant by fate, an unlikely but imperative collision of desire with consummation. The car salesman from Pasadena reached out and helped himself to four, which he promptly consumed and then reached out for another four. He was not even truly appreciating them.

Dogs of all sizes and shapes swarmed about the

server now. The silver platter caught the last of the dying sun and gleamed with otherworldly brilliance. My stomach tumbled and galloped and tumbled some more. The scent was so powerful, so substantial that I felt I was sucking the food in through my nose. I was suddenly convinced that sitting on a throne at the center of the universe there was an all-powerful, all-knowing *pig in a blanket* dispensing truth, justice, and mercy and making the celestial orbs hum. That single intoxicated thought should have been a warning that Yours Truly was about to do something rash.

The used car salesman waved the server away, Harry was offered a sampling but declined, and then the tray began to slide away from me. A single delectable peeked from the edge. Surely there would be no harm in saving such a noble food from falling to the deck. It was at this point that I found myself flying upward. There was a shout and a tug on my leash from my owner, but it was too late. With a deft flick of my tongue and a precise snap of my dependable incisors, I had secured the prize. Unfortunately, I had underestimated the force of my heft in motion, and while I maintained sound oral precision as I gulped the delectable down, I could not prevent my chest from ramming into the upright Scandinavian and his blessed silver platter. The Scandinavian grunted and folded like a pair of scissors, the tray tipped, and in an instant its contents were showering down upon corgi, affenpinscher, and Labrador retriever alike. Mojitos and frozen daiquiris spilled. Yours Truly and the other dogs found themselves rolling in a swamp of alcohol and baked delights, snout-smearing and swallowing untold quantities.

And then my leash was yanked again with an unusual severity and Harry's voice thundered my name from what seemed a very long way away.

"Randolph, stop it."

But I couldn't stop it.

"Randolph, drop it."

Nor drop it.

And he yanked again and again and finally grabbed my shoulders and pulled me back from the melee.

"We're going, Randolph," Harry said. "I don't have to tell you how disappointed I am in you."

My head sank. My pathologically optimistic tail buried itself between my legs. These were harsh words even if they were delivered on a mojito tide.

"Sometimes I don't recognize the dog that Imogen trained."

Harry apologized to the server, who held the empty silver platter in one hand and looked stunned.

"It had to be the whole tray," Harry muttered. "And I thought you were going to devour that Chihuahua next. All class, aren't you, fella?"

Harry dipped on one leg and tried to pretend it was the result of the ship's side-to-side motion. Then he gave another sharp yank on my leash and led us out of the crowd. We abandoned the mayhem on the Poop Deck and struck out down a passage for our quarters in the bowels of the ship. Someone was right behind us and wanted Harry's attention.

"Excuse me," called a short woman in a blazer holding a clipboard. This was the cruise director, Melody Buttermold, whose smiling visage I had seen plastered on posters all over the ship. It was Miss Buttermold's duty to offer structured programs to those passengers who might fall into a dark well of despair lest they find one moment of their lives unscheduled. Harry and his dog did not fall into this category, but we were still clearly in Miss Buttermold's sights.

"I'm so sorry to disturb you, I know you have a discipline problem on your hands," she said, gesturing at me.

"Randolph likes to embarrass himself," Harry said, steadying himself against the passage wall and trying to look respectable.

"Melody Buttermold," the cruise director said, extending her hand. "I'm the cruise director."

Miss Buttermold gave a girlish curtsy. "Here for your entertainment," she said and then presented Harry with a canary-yellow sheet.

"This is the schedule and I've got a gap to fill." She tapped the paper. Miss Buttermold pronounced the word *gap* as if it were an existential hazard or a dread-inducing disease.

"A gap?" Harry asked.

"Yes," she said. "I had an accountant scheduled to deliver a lecture on turning your pet's terminal cancer into a tax deduction, but he fell through and now I've got a gap. Our passengers demand value for their cruise dollars. A gap is unacceptable."

"I'm sorry to hear that," Harry said.

"Don't be. As the Chinese say, crisis is another word for opportunity. That is why I've tracked you down and want to give you an opportunity," Miss Buttermold said. "I know it's last minute and feel free to say no, but one of your friends, Mr. Temple—he's in the presidential suite—"

The cruise director said these last two words with extreme reverence.

"—suggested that you'd be absolutely perfect as a fill-in."

Harry looked confused. "I don't know anything about taxes," my owner said.

Miss Buttermold laughed and rested her hand on my owner's arm—the one that was not occupied in keeping him steady and respectable looking.

"Of course not, but he did say that you are an expert mosaicist—I hope that's the right word—and would be happy to teach a class on memorializing a dog in mosaic. Pet owners love that kind of thing—it makes art useful. It's just an hour. This Wednesday."

Harry looked doubtful.

"We already have a delightful woman—a renowned pet portraitist from New York—teaching a similar course in oils and watercolors."

Harry started to shake his head no.

"We'll reimburse half your passage," Miss Buttermold offered.

"It's a deal," Harry said.

"And we'll throw in a personalized Pet Wellness Compliance Officer."

"A what?" Harry asked.

"A Pet Wellness Compliance Officer." Miss Buttermold repeated the ungainly moniker and pointed at me. "For him. No offense, but some of our top pet experts have already made a few comments."

"About Randolph?" Harry asked.

Miss Buttermold nodded gravely. "There seems to be universal agreement that Rudolph could use some strict dictary enforcement."

Harry looked at his feet. "I guess I've been a little slack with his diet," he confessed. "You see, we're on our own, and there's a great Chinese place around the corner. They deliver. Randolph likes the ribs and the dumplings and the spring rolls with duck sauce."

My mouth began to copiously water as the mention of these delectables evoked a Pavlovian response.

Miss Buttermold said nothing at first, and Harry's recitation of my menu was brought to a sudden halt by the sheer force of her moral indignation.

"There's no excuse, I know," Harry said. "Randolph deserves better."

I could think of nothing better than a wholesome array of Asian specialties, but Harry's contrition or rather his sellout of Yours Truly won the cruise director over. Harry didn't even defend me by mentioning that I had an unusually wide rib cage, which could easily suggest added pounds.

"Don't you worry," Miss Buttermold said. "It's nothing the Pet Wellness Compliance Officer can't fix. He'll whip Rudolph into shape in no time."

Then Miss Buttermold looked at me again and reassessed.

"At least he'll get the healthy lifestyle process started," she said.

Healthy lifestyle. These two words had an icy ring to them that gravely affected Yours Truly's peace of mind, especially when they were delivered by a woman so thin as to be emaciated and possibly in need of medical attention, and whose eyes gleamed with the manic fever of someone for whom every calorie was the enemy and every doughnut a confectionary booby trap on the high road to nutritional salvation. Her sheer efficiency of care was threatening my leisure.

Harry might be profoundly incompetent in his feeding and walking duties, but my Labrador nature could accept such weaknesses and failings. It is brutal efficiency a dog cannot tolerate—we know only too well what lies at the end of that approach to the inherent messiness of life: a kennel, a lethal injection, a whimper and permanent darkness for us, while human streets remain free of the inconvenience of having my homeless brethren underfoot. *Healthy lifestyle* indeed. I huffed at the thoughtlessness of this much-bandied-about term like Orwell stewing over Politics and the English Language. I thought: *As if to read and enrich one's spirit, soul, and gray matter somehow does not rate unless it is being done on a treadmill or in between bouts with a Thigh-Master. This woman's ethic would have had Emily Dickinson out jogging along with all the other great literary gimps, recluses, and asthmatics, aspirating wheat germ instead of poetry.* I huffed again. Unfortunately, the cruise director mistook the noise for weight-related respiratory trouble.

"What's wrong with him?" Miss Buttermold asked.

"He just does that sometimes."

"I wouldn't wait another minute to get him on the path to wellness and lifestyle change," Miss Buttermold said. She added, almost as if whispering a reminder to herself, "Check what accommodations we have if one of our canine guests were to pass."

Coffins and cold storage awaited their human passengers, but the implication was that Yours Truly would be indecorously heaved overboard if he were to die aboard ship snout burrowed in a buffet tray. I huffed again.

"I think it's serious, poor thing," Miss Buttermold said. The cruise director pointed us in the direction of my salvation and headed off to find other idle passengers to terrorize.

FORTUNATELY FOR MY BAT-tered sense of self, the Pet Wellness Compliance Officer was not behind his desk in the corner of a lounge area on Deck 13. A sign informed visitors that Jock Johnson—no doubt a spry specimen oozing wellness—would return the next morning.

Even Harry seemed relieved. "I guess we'll fix you tomorrow then," he said.

An unhappy choice of words, but I made no objection.

We crossed the lounge and walked beneath a banner that read: WITH SEDADOG™ YOUR CRUISE WILL NEVER END. I had seen advertisements for Sedadog™ on television and been appalled, but not surprised, to find a pharmaceutical company diving into the lucrative world of pet care with an anti-anxiety medication. If small children could be routinely sedated and otherwise dazed by the pharmacopoeia, why not dogs? A small monitor in the Sedadog™ kiosk played a video loop showing how the drug had been shaped into individual bite-sized treats that apparently no dog could resist. A commentator extolled its virtues. Sedadog™ was designed to prevent dogs from engaging in "embarrassing" and "inappropriate" behaviors such as "barking, gnawing, jumping, digging, and tail chasing." Completely harmless and nutritional, the commentator recited, and in three flavors: Beef Stroganoff, Chicken Kiev, and Cajun Shrimp. It made dogs content, and a contented dog was an obedient dog. Sedadog™ said settle down with a smile, et cetera. Despite my principled objections to the use of such medication for canines, they did look tasty. Thankfully, there were none left in the sample tray or Yours Truly might have doped himself despite his best intentions.

"God, can't they just let a dog be a dog," Harry muttered.

"They're sponsoring the cruise and, of course, I am outraged. They have a drug for everything nowadays, even normalcy," a familiar voice informed us from across the room. It was Jackson Temple, Harry's friend and benefactor, the renowned Rubens scholar and eccentric bachelor who lived in a hotel in Manhattan. A week earlier Harry had confided our need to travel south to Jackson, and he had promptly arranged the cruise. Harry had insisted on paying for our passage and as a result, while Jackson had ended up in the presidential suite, we of limited means had ended up with a cabin in the bowels of the ship wedged between college coeds and a group of compulsive quilters on their way to learn the needle secrets of the Mesoamerican Indians.

"Sponsoring?"

"Isn't anything safe from selling?" Jackson complained. "Of course, they're sly and make it seem that it's all for our benefit: the drugs, the celebrities, the pet specialists."

"Celebrities?"

"Haven't you seen them?" Jackson asked. "There's that absurd Dog Mutterer, Milton Tabasco, and his wife, Kitty, from cable—the one who uses something called 'a hushed Tourette's-syndrome-based approach' to communicate with animals. And then there are the three monks from that other show *Dog Is God Spelled Backward*."

"I've seen those guys—they're very good with dogs."

"I wouldn't believe everything I saw on the tube. They can do magic in the editing room. The monks are also billed as fun loving and reverent, but I've spotted two of them skulking about the ship, cursing like sailors and looking downright sullen. You know, besides training dogs they make fudge and an orange schnapps implicated in half a dozen fraternity mishaps. Maybe their dark arts have finally caught up with them."

"I didn't know that you watched TV, Jackson," Harry said.

"I don't need to. I read. You can learn all you need about these people by reading," Jackson said. "Well, at least their fudge is delicious. The maple walnut is the best. The dark chocolate supreme is a close second. You can't argue with fudge. Everything else in the world might be wrong, but you can't argue with fudge or an excellent cheese for that matter. The point, my young friend, is that we are aboard a pet-friendly cruise that is really a goods-and-services hawkfest in disguise. I suppose it's the way of the world today that everything has a dollar sign attached and must be cross-branded, exhaustively marketed, and exploited from every angle, but really, what was wrong with the old unencumbered pleasures of being a passenger on a distinguished ship sailing toward the tropics?"

"Most of these passengers are probably happy it's this way," Harry said. "You know how people love their celebrities and buying things."

"And that is exactly the problem," Jackson said. "They don't know any better and they don't care to know any better."

Jackson sighed as if remembering the gilded age of the transatlantic liner with its oak-paneled staterooms and chandeliered luxury.

"Don't forget that dinner is formal tonight, Harry. At least some traditions remain," Jackson said. "I have arranged for you and Randolph to be at the captain's table."

Harry nodded. "Would you like to meet and go there together?" he asked.

"Go there? To dinner?" Jackson looked baffled. "Oh,

God, no. I'll be dining in my stateroom with Marlin tonight. He takes a while to settle into new surroundings, you know, and the best the ship could do for him was a dwarf palm that lists steeply to starboard. Each time the ship tilts a bit that direction, a distinct look of terror comes into the fellow's eyes. I really can't leave him alone too long."

Harry knew of Jackson's fondness for his Guatemalan tree sloth but didn't accept this explanation.

"What's the real reason?"

Jackson's voice dropped to a confidential hush. "Captain Bostitch is what you call a real character. As you know, the same can be said of myself. I'm afraid it is a law of nature and a rule of cruisemanship that two real characters cannot sit at the same table. Since he is the captain of this ship, who am I to impose? I don't want to prejudice you, but Captain Bostitch is also a bit of a maniac. I have traveled with him before down to the Antarctic on one of those excursions organized by the Naturalist Museum of New York. He is a perfectly capable seaman from a long line of perfectly capable, even extraordinary, seamen, but he lives under the influence of a strange Ahab-like obsession."

"He's not actually chasing down a whale," Harry said.

"Not a whale. Though he backed over one in the North Atlantic," Jackson said. "In Captain Bostitch's case he is obsessed with pirates. Not the shabby Somalian kind. The pirates he cares about are the ones up and down the South American coast and, of course, the Caribbean. In my opinion they're mostly drug runners and fishermen whose generational livelihood has been gutted by the global fishing trade, but according to Bostitch many are former colonial bureaucrats and civil servants who have taken to sea to supplement their ruined pensions. It's quite an image, an old mid-level pencil pusher heaving a cutlass or, I suppose nowadays, toting a machine gun. But he's an old British Empire man, our Captain Bostitch. Believes that the universe holds itself together on Greenwich Mean Time, and pirates work nicely into his virtue-of-empire equation. He even has a particular nemesis, the aptly named Phillip G. Marlborough, who is rumored to run a hedge fund and sail out of the Caymans. Bostitch is on the hunt for Marlborough."

"I can't wait for dinner," Harry said.

The lounge was empty with the exception of a few passengers scattered among overstuffed armchairs in a pre-dinner, post-bon-voyage-party lull, but suddenly loud, angry voices rose from the open staircase at the end of the room that descended to a lower deck.

"It's one of those monks," Jackson said. "I told you they were surly."

Surly was a kind word for the kind of language that reached the sensitive Labrador ears of Yours Truly. The monk's vocabulary was supplemented by the colorful language of his still-invisible antagonist.

"Milton Tabasco," Jackson remarked. "Using his trademark Tourette's approach on his television rival no doubt. We are witnessing a ratings war in the flesh."

The two men were climbing the stairs as they argued. A moment later they appeared: a gray-cowled monk with narrow features and large eyes and a deeply tanned man in a florid pink shirt with a giant yellow bird spilling down the front. They were so immersed in their argument that they didn't seem to notice anyone else in the room. The monk had a finger an inch away from Tabasco's nose. Instead of blocking the challenge, Tabasco's arms were thrown wide as if he were inviting an assault from the monk.

"Oh," the monk mocked. "Classic vulnerable belly display signaling lack of fear—or is it trust?"

The monk suddenly noticed that they were not alone and immediately fell silent.

"I wouldn't trust you as far as I could throw you," Tabasco said. He seemed about to say something else, but then his eyes flickered over the room and he, too, registered that there were people listening. "Go back to fudge and booze and leave the dogs to me. And whatever you do, Brother, don't forget what I told you. A man is only as good as his plan and a plan needs a man."

The monk didn't seem pleased that Tabasco had continued talking. He motioned for Tabasco to stop. Instead, Tabasco played explicitly to the crowd.

"Nothing to see, folks," he boomed with false

bonhomie that barely covered up the pair's seething tempers. "Just a little friendly professional rivalry."

It was an awkward exchange and an awkward recovery made even more so by what happened next. Tabasco left the monk and headed straight for me, tutting, clicking, cursing, muttering—his odd Tourette's syndrome approach in full force and directed at Yours Truly. I did not know whether to stand firm or run away. There was something ridiculous about Tabasco. He sounded like a cross between a Kalahari Bushman and a logorrheic madman detailing a conspiracy theory with a nervous tic that made his head dart forward every few syllables as if he were trying to spit gravel out of his mouth but couldn't spit fast enough.

It was quite a performance, but there was also something strangely hypnotic in it and I found myself losing first a sense of time and then space as Tabasco droned on saying nothing with such stunning conviction. And then I began to sense that he wasn't saying nothing after all. It wasn't English that was coming out his mouth—at least not proper English—but it was some kind of language that I found myself beginning to understand and obey. He wanted me to sit, I sat. He requested that I lift my front paw, I did so. Next it was a walk across the room. After that a brief jog. It was unclear what was going on, but I was no longer master of myself while Tabasco spoke. Then, just as I felt my body responding to another command, a familiar voice broke the spell.

"Amazing," Harry said.

"It's nothing," Tabasco replied in what I suspected was a rare moment of humility.

"No, it's really something," Harry said. "Randolph never listens to anyone."

I resented this appraisal since I consider myself an attentive dog and, if anything, am often embarrassed by my hereditary tendency to please humans—the tiresome drill sergeant of subservience that howls at any dereliction of canine duty. I would have been more annoyed, but Tabasco's methods had made me woozy and I sat down heavily on my haunches.

"He is an unusual dog," Tabasco said.

"You don't have to be kind," Harry said, continuing his winning streak.

"No, I mean that in the best possible way," Tabasco said. "Even my competitor might see it. Though I doubt it."

The monk had joined us. He looked down at me with a critical eye. I had wanted to give both Tabasco and the monk a good snout-stamping sniff to get a sense of these celebrities' characters, but, unfortunately, my olfactories were still overwhelmed by the slurry of *pigs in a blanket* that clung to my fur and nostrils and impaired the reception and analysis of any new smells.

"I'm not sure I see what you see," the monk said.

"I'm not surprised," Tabasco said. "This is not an

orthodox dog. His finest qualities will be invisible to
most eyes."

The monk ignored the comment. He reached
down, took my chin in his hand, and tilted it toward the
ceiling.

"He's a standard black Labrador. Amiable, tending
to fat—in his case, to very fat—silly tongue-lolling
mouth, a vacant but happy expression."

Of course, the monk was right about the surface of
things. I have the challenge of being unable to express
anything with my stone-dead face, which is totally inca-
pable of carrying any nuance. My eyes are cruise-control
set on perpetual goodness and my tail on vacuously
happy. I am a prisoner in my body no less than any
human—rich of depth in spirit and imagination—who
has had the misfortune of losing facial control and
speech, staring and drooling, never to smile or answer
back.

The monk dropped my chin and pointed at my paw.
"Give me your paw," he demanded.

I did nothing of the sort.

The monk frowned. "Either he's very stupid, totally
untrained, or, worse, directly disobedient and untrain-
able."

"Beyond the reach of your salvation?"

"I'm afraid so," the monk said. "A hopeless case."

The hopeless case could not stifle a huff and a full-
body shiver.

"He doesn't like that one bit," Jackson said. "I think you've got a heretic in our Randolph."

"Oh, he's a pleasant enough dog, I just don't see the depths my friend Tabasco does," the monk said. "But that's not my business. I'm a behaviorist. I work from the outside in when I train a dog. Don't tell me what you think they're thinking or feeling, just tell me what they're doing and I'll put a stop to it. In my opinion, a dog is basically a sophisticated machine that makes us believe it has emotions and thoughts when really it's just responding to cues and incentives in very predictable ways. I leave the mystical mumbo jumbo to Tabasco. I appreciate dogs, but I know their limits. And above all please don't suggest that they have souls. Ashes to ashes. Dogs to dust."

"Perhaps we're just machines then, too," Jackson said.

A knowing look came across the monk's face as if he had heard this line many times before and had memorized the response. "As far as the plumbing and circuitry go, you may be right. We're biological machines," the monk said. "But the difference is free will. Free will is what gives us legs for eternity unlike our mammalian relatives. Free will."

The monk repeated the last two words with particular emphasis.

"Those two words change everything," he went on. "Because it means we do the choosing. We decide to go right or left, up or down, and, most important, we decide whether to do good or to do evil."

Tabasco shook his head. "Not that again," he said. "Free will's a joke. It's something we made up to make ourselves feel better. Good and evil, what's that? The more I work with animals, the less I believe in good and evil. There are no absolutes. We're the ones who need to put the meaning into things. Animals just accept things the way they are. A dog would never need to build heaven, because he's already living in one."

"And see, there you go again with your old the-animals-always-know-best routine," the monk said. "Free will, fellas. Build your understanding around free will and everything else in our broken world makes instant sense."

Harry was only dimly engaged in the conversation. I knew him well. He had not liked the harsh things the monk had said about me but rather than make a scene, he had retreated to a place just beyond anyone's reach where the necessity to do battle was removed by the wider concerns of beauty. His artistic sensibilities were transfixed now. The water outside the floor-to-ceiling windows on the starboard side shimmered brilliantly to the horizon. The sun was almost finished settling into the orange cradle of the west. A buoy slid past a few hundred yards away tilting on the swells. A cluster of gulls burst upward past the windows. White sails and orange spinnakers marked a distant regatta.

"Free will," Harry echoed absently. "I like it."

Tabasco and the monk departed from us. They were smiling and acting the part of friendly rivals now, but they left a scent in their wake that made me shudder. It must have been powerful to penetrate through the fragments of *pigs in a blanket* plastered to my whiskers and snout. The best I can do now is describe it this way: One moment the scent is of a slab of the finest chocolate slowly melting in a double boiler with a pat of butter; the next moment, ammonia sears your nose. It was, I supposed, the scent of great personal charm masking the most naked and cutthroat ambition.

It was a dangerous smell.

TWO HOURS LATER HARRY and I arrived in the Aurora Borealis, the smallest and most exclusive of the ship's five dining rooms. The Aurora Borealis was perched high at bridge level and right beneath and behind the smokestacks.

This was the dining room assigned to the captain, the occupants of the high-priced suites, and any celebrities who happened to be on board. As with most of the upper portions of the *Nordic Bliss,* an entire side of the room was glass, but at this hour the glass was evenly black with night except for a few distant pinpoints of yellow light that I supposed were hamlets along the Jersey Shore.

It was a strange feeling for this Manhattan dog to feel the constant throbbing of the ship's engines, be reminded of the dark, cold fathoms of water beneath us teeming with strange, likely ravenous, aquatic beings, and know that the mighty Atlantic, ruin of many a fine man and dog, stretched out around us on all sides. Still, shipboard life—like all of life really—is often about ignoring such things and concentrating instead on the warm, comfortable certainties around us like the cream carpet, the sound of fine china clattering about happily, and the distinct aroma of trout amandine.

My owner was appropriately attired in a dark suit punctuated by a red tie. The suit had been purchased with Imogen a long time ago during a dark, artistically uncertain period when Harry had actually considered a professional career working with the clock punchers and cubiclists instead of bohemianism and painting. The tie had been borrowed from his brother-in-law, Tony, the Scottish banker, long-suffering husband of Harry's sister, Iberia, and comfortably numb father of the Labrador-hostile, ear-pulling child-menace, Haddy McClay.

Yours Truly, his whiskers now smelling of French lavender, had been thoroughly scrubbed of any traces from the *pigs in a blanket* debacle and had been permitted to go "leashless." This was a baby step in an experiment of shipboard freedom that Harry had promised to expand if I behaved myself. He had even delivered a short lecture on leashlessness, which I listened to attentively. Certainly other than powder puffs borne as accessories by silk-draped heiresses, aging grande dames, and movie stars, dogs were traditionally unwelcome on cruise ships. Not on this particular trip. A brochure had been distributed when we had boarded that afternoon outlining the "rights and responsibilities" of pets and their owners on the *Nordic Bliss*—leashlessness was actually recommended for calm dogs who were also large enough not to slip overboard beneath the rails.

Jackson was right about cruising being different from its vaunted and elegant past. The ship boasted a rock-climbing wall, a karaoke bar, and a 3-D theater. Flat-screen televisions lined many of the lounges, and the interior design of the ship did not suggest taste and class so much as it said *Let's drink frozen alcoholic concoctions and wear Hawaiian shirts*. But still some nautical elements remained. The decks were named in the traditional fashion. There was the Lido Deck where the midnight buffet was to be held every night, and, of course, the Poop Deck.

It goes without saying that the Poop Deck is not supposed to have anything to do with the product of a Number 2 biological function. The word *poop*, in the nautical context, comes from the French *la poupe*, which means "aft" or "stern." Aboard sailing ships, the Poop Deck was a raised deck at the rear of the vessel from which the helmsman steered. Later the Poop Deck lost this function when ships were steered from bridges nearer the front of the vessel.

In the case of the *Nordic Bliss* the important thing to remember is that the tidy and forward-thinking Scandinavians had constructed a special sandbox dog run in which animals were meant to perform their Numbers, but already that system was beginning to fail. My brethren had unanimously chosen the Poop Deck as the place for their business since it offered a little something for every type: discretion for the *Foliage Finder* beneath strategically placed palms, wide-open spaces for the brazen *Squat-and-Drops,* and even a patch of rough-looking pavement for those inveterate city dogs, the *Asphalt-Onlys*. In this way language evolves to accommodate reality.

Harry and I were late for dinner and waited for the maître d' to lead us to our table. The rest of the ship might have been inelegant, but the Aurora Borealis was a throwback to the heady days of transatlantic crossings. Chandeliers hung above each table. The fabrics and colors were of the highest quality. Delicate arrangements of fuchsia, wild roses, and orchids decorated the centers of each table. Diners were dressed in their finest. All the dogs were expertly groomed.

The eyes of the restaurant followed my tall owner and his squat charge across the length of the room until we reached a table in the far corner. Objectively he is a handsome fellow, my Harry, a twenty-something former water polo player who despite his abysmal dietary habits and his refusal to exercise has not gained an excess pound or lost the striking features of his youth. This and his gentle, caring, and thoughtful nature make him a frequent target of feminine affection against which I am self-appointed to defend him lest his loyalty to my mistress, Imogen, be unduly tested.

Seven people were seated around the table. I immediately identified Captain Bostitch from the shock of silver hair, the wild obsessive eyes, and the blazingly white dress uniform. Beside him sat Mrs. Captain Bostitch, also white-haired but as soft as the captain was severe. The monk from earlier had been joined by another monk from the television trio. This man also wore the gray habit with a rope belt and leather sandals, but unlike the first monk he had a dark black beard that came to a sharp point and made him look menacing even though his face was set to perma-smile. Milton Tabasco sat next to the monks. Tabasco was dressed in a tuxedo with a rakishly tilted bow tie covered with sequined dog biscuits. Beside him sat a woman who can only be described as a kind of human sequin.

This was Kitty Tabasco, whose surgically enhanced beauty screamed out like a cry for help. There was an antic desperation in the injection-smoothed forehead, the odd teal-colored eyes, the inflated lips, and the frozen bosom. Hers was a beauty of the sort that was so blatantly artificial, it made everyone around her feel like a guilty party to the lie. She had, no doubt, been a beautiful woman once, but now she was only an anxious mask waiting for worse to come.

Sitting next to Kitty like her younger version and

a twist of the knife was Zest Kilpatrick, the effervescent and attractive Channel Eight News reporter who had not too long before announced her fondness for Harry.

As if things couldn't get odder or more uncomfortable, there was an aggressive-looking monkey standing in the middle of the table cleaning out its ear with a salad fork.

The maître d' left as if he were stranding us on Devil's Island.

"Harry," Zest exclaimed and bounced to her feet to kiss him on the cheek and give his hand a pump. "What are *you* doing here?"

She didn't give Harry a chance to answer, instead turning to our table companions who ten minutes earlier were unknown to her but were now her best friends.

"Everyone, this is Harry. Harry is a famous artist or at least he's going to be. He just finished a marvelous work for the United Nations. It was on all the news outlets including mine. And this is his dog, Randy."

I should have expected this indignity from someone who pays little attention to detail and who especially disliked me for putting myself between her and my owner during a previous amorous advance. If ever I grow vocal cords I will become a voice for the voiceless.

The table nodded more or less in unison at Harry,

and he nodded back and took his seat beside Zest. Yours Truly assumed a defensive position ready to intercede against the aggressive reporter.

"I'm here with Jackson Temple," Harry said. "What are you doing here?"

"I'm here on assignment of course," Zest said. "They gave me a camera guy and an audio guy and told me to do a 'puff' piece about dogs, lovers, and exotic destinations."

She dropped her voice to confidential, but it still sounded like she was reporting in a hurricane.

"To be totally, a hundred percent, completely honest with you," Zest said. "I think they thought that I needed a break, that I was close to burnout, which is so totally untrue. But it's funny seeing you here. Too funny. Because if I am suffering from burnout, you know you're to blame. You're the nut in my fruitcake."

"Me?"

"Of course."

"Why?"

"Never mind. I'm being an idiot. Anyway, we've got some fabulous footage already. Did you know that there are more than one hundred dogs aboard and one hundred pet product companies represented? It's awesome," Zest said. "You missed the appetizer. It was herring and onions. I ate yours. Yum."

Zest delivered an overly cozy smile to Harry.

One of the waiters, an exceedingly slender, odd-looking Scandinavian, had arrived with Zest's main course—Swedish meatballs—and dropped them in front of the reporter with a plunk after shoving his arm past her face, eclipsing the flirtation.

"Was that necessary?" Zest complained, but the waiter was gone. The march of the meatballs continued, and soon the table was steaming with this delicacy of the North Country. I would have felt deprived but the same brusque waiter returned and placed an adequate bowlful at my feet. I would have thanked him with a snout swipe, but he had already disappeared.

Not everyone at the table was satisfied. Captain Bostitch, who had been watching the proceedings in silence, suddenly sprang to volcanic life.

He wanted salt and lots of it.

This blustery, sun-parched sea dog, descendant of Victorian naval officers, with a visage that might have been chiseled out of the white cliffs of Dover, did not like how his Swedes had cooked their meatballs.

"A bland race the lot of them," he grumbled. "If it weren't for their ingenuity with furniture and their sound hygienic practices, they'd be finished."

In another age Captain Bostitch, lately of Southampton, England, would have found an avenue for his frustrations in the thrice-weekly flogging of his crew, the parsimonious distribution of the rum rations, and the occasional keelhaul. Instead, like all of us, he had been born into an era that values risk reduction and social sensitivities over high-volume heroics of the man-versus-sea variety. Thus, Captain Bostitch was a man constrained, a figure of legendary possibility forced to work in the hospitality industry. Still, he was a man around whom passengers instinctively trod lightly. Even Milton Tabasco knew that he was dealing with a loose cannon.

"Damn jackanapes," Captain Bostitch muttered and savaged his salad.

"What should we expect in terms of weather, Captain?" Tabasco ventured gently. "Smooth sailing?"

"Red sky at night, sailor's delight, sir," Captain Bostitch pronounced. "Red sky in morning, sailor take warning."

"Which is it, Captain?"

"Keep an eye out, my good man. The sea, she can change in an instant. So keep an eye out and one hand for the rigging," the captain said as one of the efficient though strategically unresponsive Scandinavians passed the table. "Salt, you Swedish blighters, bring me salt."

"I believe it is the former. The radar tells us a high-pressure system is on the way," Mrs. Captain Bostitch said to Tabasco and then lowered her voice confidentially. "My little rogue wave doesn't like calm seas."

Mrs. Captain Bostitch then addressed her husband, who was craning his neck looking for salt. "Larry, sweetheart, you know what the doctor has said about salt and your arteries."

Captain Bostitch glared at his wife as if he had just spied an iceberg off the starboard side.

"He's hypertensive," Mrs. Captain Bostitch told the table, then quickly reassured anyone who might have doubts about his competency on the bridge. "But there is no reason to think he couldn't handle any nautical emergency."

"Were I only alive in the age of sail when the salt on the wind would have been enough for me. I would have licked it off my whiskers," the captain mumbled. As Mrs. Captain Bostitch waved away the last of the attendant Swedes, one of whom bore a saltshaker, the captain realized that he was defeated and dug into his unsalted Swedish meatballs. Bostitch's command, the modern marvel *Nordic Bliss,* cruised on guided southward by software and satellites.

Tabasco, ever the entertainer, realizing that the only competition for verbal dominance at the table had now been muted, regaled us with tales of intelligent animals and their moronic owners. Captain Bostitch ate in vanquished silence. The two monks seemed to have no problem with the lightly salted fare and asked for seconds. Kitty's monkey broke another champagne flute on its head and no one reacted, on her instruction.

"That's a classic attention-seeking behavior. It's better if you don't say anything," Kitty cautioned. "Chitlin can get a teensy bit violent—his formative years were spent with a band of tourist-robbing street monkeys in Mumbai who eventually killed the premier. We were there on a television shoot, *Taming the Dogs of India,* heard the poor thing's tale of woe, bribed the right officials, and spirited him out of the country disguised as a chapati pan a day before he was scheduled to be executed."

The unflappable Tabasco ignored his wife's story and her advice and aimed a volley of his trademarked Tourette's syndrome nonsense language at Chitlin.

"Typecast...piss pepper...Strait of Gibraltar," Tabasco hissed.

The monkey stopped, dropped a third champagne flute, scratched his tiny simian chin, scooped up a saltshaker hidden beneath the centerpiece, and hurled it at Tabasco's head. The projectile missed the Dog Mutterer but ricocheted off a Swede and dropped into a platter of meatballs on its way to a far table.

"You little bastard," Tabasco muttered.

"There goes the salt." Captain Bostitch sighed in a way that suggested that he had been delivered yet more evidence of our journey's dismal future. This did little to inspire Yours Truly, who was still getting used to the ship's disquieting rocking beneath his four sensitive paws.

"Where's the third man? The fat monk?" Tabasco asked the monk from earlier whose full name was Brother Phillipus of Antioch but who liked to be called Gary.

"Brother Timothy Sextus?" Gary responded as if

this were an odd question. The second monk feigned absorption in his dinner napkin, which he had folded into the shape of a bird.

"He's the man," Tabasco said. "The Numero Uno of your three musketeers."

"Brother Timothy has chosen to stay in our cabin fasting and praying for the success of the singles pet cruise sponsored by Sedadog™."

Captain Bostitch groaned. "Is that what they're calling our voyage?"

"I'm sorry, Captain, I suppose I fell into corporate-speak."

"Do you know what the happiest years of my life were?" Captain Bostitch asked the table.

Mrs. Captain Bostitch reached over and patted her husband's arm, but he continued anyway.

"Have you ever heard of solitary confinement such as may be imposed on a prisoner during a time of war, sirs? Have you ever heard of the bamboo sliver torture?"

"Larry, please don't go on so. There's Baked Alaska for dessert."

This brightened our captain until he noticed that the New York Great Dane Appreciation Society was forming a conga line with its human and animal members.

"Good God," he said.

"It will only be a week, dear, and then you'll get your

ship back," Mrs. Captain Bostitch whispered. "Look, here comes dessert."

The lights were dimmed and then to general applause a small army of Nordic waiters streamed single-file out of the kitchen holding the great white flaming mounds on platters with sparklers. They created a figure eight around the tables in the center of the room, pushed through the conga line, and then retreated to the kitchen to extinguish the desserts and cut up the pieces.

A striking blonde arrived at our table with the dessert tray. This woman had served the table intermittently throughout the evening, and each time she had approached I noticed two distinct reactions from the Tabascos: Milton smiled with a self-conscious, naughty-boy charm; Kitty frowned and stewed.

This time, however, the waitress leaned over the Dog Mutterer, dangling her profound Nordic bosom as she set the Baked Alaska down.

"As deep and wide as the fjords," Captain Bostitch pronounced as if he had never heard of a sexual harassment lawyer.

For his part, Tabasco stared up admiringly at the woman with the look of a man who believes that he can enjoy the fruits of any crime without fear of prosecution.

"That does it," Kitty Tabasco shouted. "I have put up with all the tomcatting I can take from you, Milton Tabasco. You're despicable."

Tabasco looked surprised but not particularly worried. Kitty stood up, seized a platter of sliced mangos from out of another server's hands, and slid its contents into the Dog Mutterer's lap.

"That should cool you down for a while, hot pants," Kitty said as tears began to stream down her face from her frozen eyes and her taut, unmoving brow. "I'm so tired. So damn tired…"

Then she turned to the table and apologized.

"I'm sorry, everyone," she said. "He's so charming on the surface, but if you had to live with him like I do then you'd understand. You'd see how cruel he is. How he expects so much and gives so little back."

Whatever else Kitty Tabasco was feeling, one distinct scent was that of genuine sadness—the kind of romantic regret and nostalgia that mourns individual moments like the death of something living. It was a smell like burning cedar and hot pepper.

Then Kitty lifted her carefully constructed face with its fierce rivulets of mascara-stained tears and marched out of the dining room.

"It isn't ideal," she sniffed as she went.

Chitlin delivered a single high-pitched shriek in Milton Tabasco's direction, hopped off the table, and trailed after his mistress.

"Green bean…martinet…Laplander," Tabasco said with his trademarked Muttering.

"I feel like I should go after her," Zest said, but did not budge from her chair.

"I wouldn't worry about it," Tabasco said. "I guess I've always been better with dogs than women. Anyway, she's tough as nails. Give her five minutes and she'll forget all about it. In the meantime, what's your story, pretty lady?"

BOTH HARRY AND I FELT drawn to the outside decks after our first dinner. Harry did not ask for any company, but Zest Kilpatrick pretended that he had and then declined the non-offer, saying she had footage to review with the crew and needed to make them feel better anyway because they had not been invited to dine with her in the Aurora Borealis.

Harry found an exit right outside our dining room.

"Outstanding," my owner said as he stepped onto the deck. The moon, near full, trimmed everything in silver. The ocean was jumping with light. Swells rose to catch the moon and then sank back into black satin. I still felt very far from home and the familiar world of sidewalks, dusty dog runs, and that grand, civilized Central Park—the crown of our narrow island—but for a moment the sheer immensity of the ocean and sky was too much for me and struck so much awe that had I had tear ducts, I would have cried with joy. Instead my overly eager tail wagged.

"Happy to be outside, Randolph?" Harry asked. "I bet you are. There's only so much of this close-quarters shipboard life that a man can take."

We began to walk aft. Harry had taken off his tie and was dragging it along the rail.

"You know, she'd better have a very good reason for leaving us," he mused. I knew he was speaking of our mistress because of the way he pronounced *she*. No one else was meant when he said *she* that way.

"She could have brought me in on it," Harry said. "She should have let me know."

He had stopped at the railing between lifeboats and wrapped the tie into a tight ball around his clenched fist.

"She should have let me make up my mind. She should have let me protect her."

I took a more circumspect view because I had seen firsthand what dark forces Imogen had been up against. Harry was chivalrous and lonely, but Imogen had been practical. She had known that the people who were interested in her fortune would have hurt him had she not done such a good job of leaving us out of it. Now things were different. She was including us once again. Perhaps she knew now that practicality and common sense had their shortcomings. Harry and I had suffered in her absence. My diet had followed Harry's into recklessness and excess. My lower natures had gained more power over me than they should have. It had been a

year and a half of too much television and too little outside life.

Now sitting beside him and resting my chin on the
chill steel bar of the railing, I found myself grateful for
this momentary pause. I felt middle age in my bones
and the damp sea air making things stiff and inflex-
ible. Naturally my mind drifted toward poetry and the
great Victorian poet of man and the sea, Alfred Lord
Tennyson:

> There lies the port: the vessel puffs her sail:
> There gloom the dark broad seas...
> The long day wanes: the slow moon climbs:
>   the deep
> Moans round with many voices. Come, my
>   friends,
> 'Tis not too late to seek a newer world.
> Push off, and sitting well in order smite
> The sounding furrows; for my purpose holds
> To sail beyond the sunset, and the baths
> Of all the western stars, until I die.

The great ocean liner drummed on. Far below I
heard the waves cresting and crashing against the hull,
and suddenly I *believed*—possibly for the first time
since Imogen went away—that we were really getting
somewhere and that there would be an end point to our
long journey. We had pushed off and were smiting the

waves with our oars and there would be a beach upon which to land and she would be there waiting.

"Come on, Randolph," Harry said. "Let's keep walking."

He had no leash to tug since I was temporarily unrestrained. It was a good feeling to walk beside him. It gave me the momentary illusion of being equals. No one was about as we made our way aft to the Poop Deck. There was a near-constant headwind blowing astern, but for a second or two it shifted and a strong gust blew toward us. For this reason I heard and smelled the woman before I actually saw her. It was Kitty Tabasco. The leash, I realized, worked both ways. Had I been on it, I could have dug my paws in and stopped Harry from disturbing Kitty's solitude. I could have led my owner back the way we came. Instead Harry and I rambled amiably into her grief.

Tabasco had called his wife tough as nails, but the woman we encountered hunched over the railing and sobbing into a handkerchief was as close to a broken person as I've seen or smelled. She seemed utterly oblivious to us—and as it turned out, we were not alone. A few other passengers had braved the chill night air to stroll the decks. A Cavalier King Charles spaniel sniffed Kitty's pant leg and moved on. The dog's owner, a man wearing a tuxedo, approached and asked if Mrs. Tabasco needed help.

Harry and I were near enough to hear her response.

"The kind of help I need, no one in *this* world can give."

Kitty turned her face away from her questioner and continued her sobbing. The water boiled far below her in the moonlight, churned up by the ship's powerful propellers. She extended her arm out over this abyss, released one soggy much-used handkerchief, and watched it drop down into the waves. Then she dug around in her pantsuit, emerged with a fresh one, and began the process of soaking it all over again.

"Sad," Harry whispered. We left Kitty sobbing beneath the moon and went inside.

At a huge display at the base of the stairs that led down from the Poop Deck, we learned that there were no shortage of activities inside the *Nordic Bliss:* seven dance floors, thirteen bars, five lounge-bars, two lounge-lounges, a bowling alley, the aforementioned rock-climbing wall, a twenty-meter lap pool, a jet current exercise pool, a golf driving range, two volleyball courts, a boxercise area, an ice-skating rink, a Broadway-sized theater, a movie theater, a video arcade, a toddler disco, an elementary school disco and a teen disco, a pop art gallery, a folk art gallery, five lecture halls, a waffle bar, and a wax museum.

By the time I finished reading the list of all these possibilities I was exhausted. Harry was, too. We took the elevator to the bowels of the ship, subdeck C, where our room would be the first to flood in the event of a maritime tragedy. The compulsive quilters were already asleep or, more likely, compulsively quilting in one of the lecture rooms, but the college coeds—dressed in halter tops and tight gym shorts with Greek sorority symbols billboarded across generous and athletically narrow bottoms alike—were drunk and running up and down the hall throwing wads of wet toilet paper at one another in between shots of orange schnapps and beer chasers.

Naturally, a wad flew through the air at precisely the wrong moment and struck me in the head. It stuck just behind my ears, where I could not immediately reach it or shake it off. Harry flicked the wad onto the floor.

"You're cute," one of the girls gushed at Harry. "Want to do a shot off my abs?"

Harry smiled but moved on saying nothing. We reached our door.

"Sorry about your dog," another girl said. "He's cute, too. Fat, but cute."

Harry opened the door and we slipped inside.

Our cabin consisted of a single narrow bed, a sliver of floor, a tiny television, a dresser, and a writing desk. A large steam pipe cut diagonally across the ceiling, and the bed head was crowned by half a dozen massive rivets that I assumed were vital to keeping the *Nordic Bliss* from splitting in two. Every three minutes they actually creaked. We were so far below the waterline that there was no porthole.

The bathroom was even more compact than the stateroom and showcased Nordic ingenuity. The sink folded down, as did the toilet. The shower wasn't a shower at all but a transparent, space-saving plastic cylinder that needed to be pulled down over the user from the ceiling. Once inside, the participant—because that is the best way of describing the user's level of involvement in the showering process—would control temperature and pressure by depressing bright-colored foot pedals that had no connection to universally understood colors for hot and cold. The water flowed out through a drain in the floor. Harry had attempted a shower before dinner and gotten trapped in the cylinder. He then confused the happy-faced orange pedal (signifying hot water) with the frowning-faced red pedal (signifying cold water) and a neutral-faced blue pedal (signifying scalding, potato-boiling water). Venturing a nap between the base of the bed and the miniature desk, Yours Truly had spent a few anxious moments listening to Harry's howls as his mojito-clumsy feet determined the right pedals to push.

Harry didn't attempt another shower now. Instead he stretched out on the bed and turned on the television while I wedged myself into the only vacant space on the floor. I missed the presence of Grandfather Oswald's La-Z-Boy, which dominated our living room in New York and provided my owner's permanent perch near which I typically curled in my own designated cozy corner. Still, even this strange place offered a sense of sanctuary.

There were dozens of movies playing on demand

and one single extravagant documentary for Sedadog™ that would be running until dawn. This piece was different from the one I had seen playing earlier in the lounge. The style was more cinematic (slow-motion cutaways of royal-looking dogs and light breaking through Cecil B. DeMille clouds), the tone more solemn, and the content more personal and urgent. Owners of so-called problem dogs were asked to recall the darkest days of their animals' pre-Sedadog™ lives:

"It was awful, absolutely awful," Lizzie M. of Strayhorn, Connecticut, wailed into the camera. "My God, I still have nightmares about that time. He'd be digging and digging into the carpet and I'd say stop but Bellafonte wouldn't stop and I'd say stop or I'll take away *woofypoofy*—*woofypoofy* is his favorite toy—but no response... nothing... just more digging. And one day he just looked at me with those great big almond eyes of his and I could just hear him screaming out: *Doggymama, I need help... I just can't control myself anymore...* Then I found Sedadog™. Those bite-sized treats are a winner." At this point Lizzie M. leaned into the camera and whispered, "Between you and me I wish they made them for my kids, my husband, my mother-in-law... As long as I live I'll never forget my little Bellafonte's eyes. The poor little thing wanted to change so bad, but he just couldn't do it on his own." Lizzie M. began to cry, but then got ahold of herself and smiled. "But you know I don't see that look anymore and thanks to Sedadog™, I never will again..."

Harry watched two or three testimonials and a paradisal pastiche of a golden retriever all ashimmer with sunlight running through meadows and leaping over mountain streams.

"Another dog sentenced to life on Sedadog™," Harry observed. "Better watch out, Randolph. Indiscriminate hors d'oeuvre snatching might be the slippery slope to Sedadog™. We just might have to medicate."

I knew Harry's sense of humor and sturdy underlying values well enough to know that I was not in any danger of this happening. No one in our little family thought that there was an easy road in this life or that depriving other beings of their senses for your own convenience could ever be justified. The coeds had stumbled off to one of thirteen bars or seven dance floors and the hallway was now silent. Harry, having turned the lights down and the television to the ship's nautical information channel, drifted off to sleep in his suit with Tony's red tie still wrapped around his hand and dragging down to the floor.

I could not rest. Some dogs are rugged travelers; I apparently am not. The idea of roaming free aboard the *Nordic Bliss* was indeed exciting, but at the same time certain territorial instincts within me were being battered by all this movement and I was out of sorts. It also did not help that as the hour ticked past twelve, I knew we were missing the midnight buffet—perhaps my last chance for a generous culinary sampling before the

Pet Wellness Compliance Officer, the athletically monikered Jock Johnson, got ahold of me. After that I would likely end my days on an intravenous tofu drip.

But it was not these concerns that kept me awake— it was something much more serious, though at first I couldn't guess what it was. This Labrador retriever has a twelve-hour sleep quota. Insomnia is very rare for me. Yet there I was as the hours slipped by, awake and growing anxious.

According to the nautical information channel we were traveling between twenty-five and twenty-eight knots. The video camera that captured the view from the bridge showed calm seas lit by lunar glow. I began to watch the screen obsessively, monitoring the ship's speed as if I were taking the pulse of someone who at any moment might slip into cardiac arrest. I half-expected to see a mountainous rogue wave building on the horizon and heading for the ship. I imagined it striking us, the sensation of the ship heeling over, perhaps even flipping, and then cold water roaring into the bowels of the ship, rushing down our hallway, flowing under our stateroom door, turning order into chaos and death, civility and bright, practical interior design into a saline graveyard. My body became as delicately sensitive as a seismograph. I detected every bump and lurch, expecting the alarm bells to ring at any moment and the heavy watertight doors to grind shut.

It was not like me to fear only distant possibilities, so I began to question why I might be feeling this way.

Was there something else, some threat perhaps, that I had recently encountered that made me feel vulnerable and ready to sense danger everywhere? And then, around four that morning, when all the entertainments, the bars, and the lounges had closed, the compulsive quilters and the even rowdier coeds had returned to their cabins and gone to sleep, I realized what was bothering me: It was the combined scent of Milton Tabasco and the celebrity monk who liked to be called Gary.

I have already described the scent I mean: slowly melting chocolate clashing with ammonia. Or as I translated it for myself: great personal charm concealing cutthroat ambition. At the time I couldn't be sure whose great personal charm it was and whose cutthroat ambition. But lying on the floor and sifting through scent memory as well as the events at the dinner table, I began to isolate the origin. The origin was Milton Tabasco on both counts. And then I began to think of Kitty alone on the Poop Deck shedding deep sadness, regret, and sobbing uncontrollably. The ambition that I smelled in Tabasco was dangerous—cutthroat didn't mean merely competitive. It meant violence that would be employed to attain a certain objective and clear the path of all obstacles in his way.

Kitty Tabasco was in danger from her husband, and she had known it. What she said in the dining room about Tabasco's cruelty came back to me, as did the scent of her sadness and brokenness—the kind of smell that you might find on a death row prisoner waiting for a dawn execution that will not be stayed.

But what could I do? The clock read 4:24. If I was to wake Harry, what would that accomplish? I could drag him on a walk to do my Numbers but what did I expect to find? Kitty Tabasco still leaning over the rail and sobbing six hours later? Why was I convinced that the danger was immediate?

I was also up against my old problem of communication. In other recent desperate straits I had found ways to break through to Harry without jeopardizing the illusion that his Labrador was not particularly bright (in this world of eager experimental scientists who might whisk Yours Truly off to a laboratory, to be underestimated is to remain free). I had arranged messages in Alpha-Bits and pretended that they had been authored by a spirit guide (Harry is susceptible to beliefs in the paranormal). I had even ventured onto the Internet to communicate with my owner by e-mail.

But what were my options at 4:24, now 4:25, in the morning? And then catastrophe actually seemed to strike. The watertight doors slammed shut, alarm bells began to ring, and the great engines of the *Nordic Bliss* suddenly stopped. My heart began to pound at an unhealthy clip. I second-guessed myself. Perhaps the threat was from the sea after all and I was just trying to attach a human drama to it. The televised view of the ocean from the bridge had gone blank, and all that remained was the digital counter displaying the swiftly slowing speed of the ship: *21 kts, 19 kts, 15 kts* ... They didn't want to terrorize us with images of the great wave. *12 kts, 9 kts, 7 kts* ... Then we were at zero. Standing still on the ocean on high alert. Sitting ducks.

Or at least *I* was on high alert, because it didn't sound like anyone else was stirring. Harry dropped the tie onto the floor and shifted to face the wall. With the exception of two Scandinavians walking briskly down the hall outside our room, all was silent. Minutes passed during which I expected the worst to happen. But it never did. Instead after an hour the ship trembled, the digital counter registered that we were moving once again, and the televised view reappeared showing only placid seas.

Exhausted and realizing that there was nothing to be done until morning, I fell into a deep sleep, forgetting ocean and Tabascos alike.

"HARRY, SIT WITH US." THE voice that called my owner's name was familiar and, not, as it usually was, unwelcome. Ivan Manners and Mr. Apples, his rainbow lorikeet, waved to us from a corner table dappled in brilliant early-morning sun. We were in the aptly named Sunshine Salon, one of three breakfast "nooks" into which a passenger could drop to consume enough carbohydrates to meet the annual per-capita intake for sub-Saharan Africa. The used car salesman from Pasadena was there vacuuming up his breakfast, as was a platoon of information technologists from Triangle Park. The nightmare of the early-morning hours had passed for me, and I looked forward to this new day with enthusiasm. Unused to my new environment, I had overreacted and imagined sinister doings and disasters where there had been none at all.

Harry, his tray brimming with half a dozen bagels and three strawberry smoothies, whooped at the sight of Ivan.

"Mr. Manners," Harry said. "What the hell are you doing here?"

Ivan Manners was not someone I particularly appreciated. In fact, in the past I had harbored a strong dislike for this pushy, arrogant, rotund young man who had frequently been rude to my owner (out of envy I think).

Ivan was a self-styled "ghost hunter" whose reputation for ridding the metropolitan area of troublesome spirits had grown to almost celebrity status after an appearance on one of the morning television talk shows. Harry, who had become vulnerable to things paranormal after Imogen's disappearance, had occasionally accompanied Ivan on ghost-hunting expeditions during which Yours Truly would watch two grown men, one responsible for his care and feeding, spook each other and behave like nincompoops.

But at this moment, meeting over breakfast trays (or under breakfast trays, since Harry had found canine breakfast treats upon which I could nibble), I was almost glad that Ivan and Mr. Apples were here—it supplied what that counterman in *Breakfast at Tiffany's* called "a kind of continuity with the past."

This warm feeling did not last, however.

"I saw your art show in the paper," Ivan said without bothering to answer Harry's question. "You're wasting your time, my friend. Art is dead. What we're learning about alternative universes, the spirit world, and the futility of objective reality makes art and artists obsolete, a thing of the past. You're a relic."

"Thanks for the encouragement," Harry said. "Want to answer my question?"

Mr. Apples, muttering in Farsi, his native tongue (his first owner was an Iranian taxi driver), hopped down beside me beneath the table and began to peck at my canine breakfast treats. Food is sacred, and I delivered a short, decisive growl to which Mr. Apples responded with a histrionic squawk and flutter of the wings.

"Aggressive," Ivan observed, taking a peek beneath the table. "You know they've got something for that. And they're chewable."

Harry ignored this latest plug for Sedadog™.

"So what are you doing here?"

"I, my friend, am on the cutting edge. I am exploring heretofore unexplored reaches of experience. I have been given free passage so that I can lead a group of paranormally curious passengers on a tour I am billing Haunted Curaçao."

"Sounds interesting," Harry said. "Have you ever been to Curaçao?"

Something had changed in the way my owner handled Ivan Manners. Harry had ceased being uncertain and deferential around him. There was a new confidence in his bearing. The strength that he had possessed when he had first met Imogen was returning and, moreover, it had been refined by the trial of her absence. I was glad to see it.

Ivan, however, didn't seem glad at the difference. He floundered and was unsure of himself and I recognized what I had always disliked in him: that he was a petulant, competitive child desperate for the upper hand in any situation. I chomped down decisively on the last of my canine breakfast treats.

"Curaçao," Ivan said offhandedly. "Nope, never been there. But if you're the ghost king of Manhattan, unfamiliarity is simply not an issue. I guarantee that there's something down there and we're going to find it. Dutch colonials, pirates, slaves, revolutionaries. There's bound to be an army of the restless dead. My equipment is going to go off the charts and I wouldn't be surprised if we captured several ectoplasmic events on film."

"Good luck," Harry said.

I sat up on my haunches and rested my chin on my owner's knee on the off chance that this might secure several more canine breakfast treats. He did not get the message.

Ivan finished his overstuffed western omelet and began to polish off the three chocolate-glazed doughnuts stacked in the corner of his tray. Halfway through doughnut number two, he made this blithe announcement through his chocolate-stained teeth:

"Hear about the suicide?"

"Suicide?"

"Last night," Ivan said. "When the ship stopped."

"The ship stopped?"

"Damn right it did," Ivan said. "I was doing a dry run with my group on the forward deck getting advance measurements on the Bermuda Triangle—you know that it's a quantum hiccup, a foldover in the fabric of space–time?—"

Harry shook his head.

"That's why all those ships have disappeared. They've been transported to alternative realms."

I am not a strict empiricist and am well aware that much knowledge lies beyond our senses and current lines of scientific inquiry, but when Ivan spoke this way I, too, wanted to be transported to an alternative realm far away from his blather. Harry seemed to agree, because he kept Ivan on track.

"Someone committed suicide on *this* ship *last* night?"

"Absolutely," Ivan said. "You slept through it, but I saw it."

"You saw it?"

"I exaggerate," Ivan said. "I saw the aftermath of the event and was the first person to encounter an eyewitness."

"What happened?"

"Basically some lady jumped off the Poop Deck. Some other lady saw her do it but didn't report it right away because she was drunk or something. When it finally got reported ten seconds afterward they stopped the ship for an hour. They finally figured out that there was nothing they could do since the Coast Guard chopper had arrived, a cutter was to follow, and it's not like this ship is really equipped to do a real rescue—so we sailed on."

"So she's just out there somewhere?"

"I'm sure she's dead," Ivan said. "I don't think we're in the Gulf Stream yet so that means the water's fifty degrees. Hypothermia is the cause of half the boating deaths in the United States. Average adult man or woman would be incapacitated in minutes and dead in less than an hour. Yep, she's dead."

Harry was silent for a moment as he took a while to reflect, no doubt as I did, on our own recent cold-water survival test. Then my owner asked an important question.

"Who was she?"

"Heard of Milton Tabasco?" Ivan asked. "You know, the Dog Mutterer—that freak who curses at animals on TV and acts like they can understand him?"

My canine breakfast treats suddenly wanted to climb back up my esophagus.

"It was his wife," Ivan concluded. "I think her name was Kate, Kit, something like that . . ."

"It was Kitty. Her name was Kitty," Harry said. "We had dinner at their table last night. I saw her crying afterward. She got jealous at something he did."

"*You* had dinner at their table?" Ivan demanded. "That must have been the captain's table. How did you manage to finagle your bloody way into a place at the captain's table? I was squeezing everyone I knew to get there. See and be seen. It's so important in my business. That would have been plum."

Harry shrugged.

"That's sad about Kitty," my owner said.

"It's all relative." Ivan shrugged and absorbed his third and final doughnut.

Kitty's death might have been relative to Ivan Manners whose hot tub theology posited a revolving door between the world of flesh and the world of spirit. But it was not relative for me. Every single life means something or no life means anything at all. I know this in my Labrador bones to be true, and it is confirmed by the cultivation of my reason. Kitty's life had meant something whether or not there had been someone there to comfort her on the Poop Deck. And her death and my failure to prevent that death meant something. The warning bells had been going off in my head for hours before she had jumped from the ship and my own watertight doors had been slammed shut, preparing me for a need I did not recognize and an action that I did not take.

Ivan was wiping his chocolate-smeared fingers on the edge of the table instead of on a napkin as if he were scraping excess plaster from the edge of a trowel. Mr. Apples dragged his beak across the mess, desperate to get a chocolate fix.

Ivan pointed down at Yours Truly. "By the way, he's gotten really fat."

"You think?"

"Absolutely," Ivan pronounced. "Morbidly obese. You're supposed to see their ribs. How old is he?"

"He's going to be six this fall."

"You don't get him to lose those pounds and he won't see seven," Ivan predicted and rose from his seat, leaving his tray for one of the Scandinavians to clean up. Harry bussed his own.

"I'm gonna grab me a smoke," Ivan said when we had left the Sunshine Salon. "Care to join?"

"Nope, I quit a while ago," Harry said. We left Ivan to try to look important without an audience.

Even though the voyage was billed as a pet cruise, the ship was too large to be exclusively given over to animals and their besotted owners. Passengers and dogs were free to travel anywhere on the ship, but the designated area for most pet-related activities was Deck 13, at the rear of which was the aforementioned Poop. The forward portion of Deck 13 usually featured two volleyball courts, but one of these had been converted into the sandbox that the tidy Scandinavians had assumed would serve for our Numbers. The general consensus among the dogs, however—Manhattan was represented by a large contingent of dog-run-savvy types— seemed to be that the sandbox was too litterbox-like for anyone's taste.

"I am not a cat," a Dandie Dinmont terrier har-rumphed with an Upper East Side lilt. Most of my brethren do not have the linguistic control of Yours Truly, and I am frequently at a loss to find any decent conversation—it is usually all tangents, distraction, rumor, and impulse with my brethren. Some New York dogs can be superficially sophisticated and full of their owners' prejudices and affectations, but no less distracted by distraction. For example, this Dandie Dinmont, whose name was Chester, repeated the cat line several times emphatically, but then dashed off to chase the volleyball's shadow in the adjacent court only to return to the sandbox a moment later and behave exactly like a cat.

Moving aftward from the giant litterbox, we entered the sprawling lounge where Harry and I had witnessed Milton Tabasco and Gary, the monk, fighting the day before. It was to the far corner that Harry led me now, slaloming through dozens of dogs and their owners all hurrying to various activities as if it were the first day of school. I caught a passing glance at one of my favorites from Central Park, Preposition Betwixt, also known as Posey. Posey was a silky white Labrador retriever and pit bull mix with camel-colored ears, camel patches on her head, and very kind and intelligent eyes. Her adventurous spirit had led her to explore virtually every corner of our park, and her speed ensured that no squirrel could ever feel entirely secure. Unfortunately, this same energy meant that there was never time to stop for a chat either in our beloved Manhattan or on board ship. Although I had once overheard her owner mentioning that she had a fear of thunder and fireworks, I was happy to observe that she seemed perfectly at ease on the high seas.

Unfortunately, there would be no escape for me today. Harry was determined to "save" his fat dog and Jock Johnson, Pet Wellness Compliance Officer, stood ready at his post, running shorts secured around a trim midriff and, somewhat unbelievably, a coach's whistle dangling from his neck sharing string with a stopwatch the size of a sundial. I expected this Actors' Equity fitness character to be wearing a NO PAIN NO GAIN T-shirt. Instead his personal billboard read SEDADOG EXTRA™ THE SNACK THAT CALMS AS IT THINS.

When Jock Johnson spotted me, it was like Ahab spying the white whale. Apparently, I was to become some kind of ultimate professional challenge for him.

"Houston, we have a problem," Jock Johnson announced, using that unfunny construction employed by the cheesy and imaginationless fishing for the easy laugh. It never ceases to amaze me how often humans—so confident in their own individuality—speak with what George Orwell called packaged thought, stringing entire unthinking sentences out of trite word bubbles used a thousand times before. Those who announce that they are "thinking outside of the box" are actually telling you that they will never ever get out of the box, and someone who "gives two hundred percent

effort to everything I do" doesn't understand percent-
ages. I suspected Coach Johnson would provide me
with many more such chestnuts.

"This is Randolph?" Johnson asked.

Harry nodded.

"You're gonna be my special project, aren't you,
boy," Jock Johnson said. Then he turned to Harry and
became very grave. "Bring me up to speed. What's the
profile?"

"He's got a thyroid problem."

"On medication?"

"We just started."

"Then it's yes to the question?"

"Yes."

"Anything else?"

"No."

"Let me hit you with a statistic."

"Okay."

"Nine out of ten dogs in the US of A are obese."

"Wow."

"Any idea why?"

"They eat too much."

Jock Johnson made the sound of a game show
buzzer.

"Wrong," he said. "Want to try again?"

"They have slow metabolisms?"

Johnson buzzed. "It's stress."

"Stress?" Harry asked.

Johnson nodded.

"That's right," he said. "Dogs are heavily stressed."

"About what?"

"More than most people realize," Johnson said. "They stress over their owners' expectations. They stress over their own expectations for themselves. They stress over hunting and pack techniques that they desperately try to assimilate into modern life. They stress over their doodies. They stress over their owners going away. You name it, they stress over it. And stress builds here..."

Johnson pointed at my head.

"But it ends up here..."

He indicated my generous belly.

"What can we do about it?" Harry asked.

"I don't know if you've heard about Sedadog™?"

I had seen this one coming.

"How could I not," Harry said. "It's all over everything. It's even all over your shirt."

"That's right," Johnson said, pointing at his T-shirt. "And this is Sedadog Extra™ *It Calms as It Thins*... It deals with both the stress problem with a powerful anti-anxiety med and the calorie problem with a powerful appetite suppressant. It's a double whammy. Highly effective. I'd advise—"

"We're not doing it," Harry said.

Jock Johnson was suddenly out of things to say, but he quickly recovered.

"You know what," he said. "I'm so happy that you took a stand and said what you meant."

"I feel pretty strongly about it," Harry said.

"You believe something and you said it. Kudos to you," Johnson said. Then his voice dropped. "To be totally honest with you, I'm more of a straight diet-and-exercise guy myself. It's just they pay me ten percent to get people's pets started on the meds and, hey, I've got to make a living, too."

"Right," Harry said.

"But truth be told," Johnson said. "I would be honored to work with Randolph in the 'old-school' way and get him to drop pounds."

"No drugs," Harry confirmed.

"No drugs," Johnson said. "Just blood, sweat, and tears."

I began to wish for drugs.

Then Jock Johnson reached for something on his desk and held it up to Harry. "We'll start with my secret weapon."

Johnson's secret weapon was a spongy, soap-shaped sign, bright pink with bright yellow letters, designed to attach to a dog collar.

Oh, dear, Yours Truly thought. I took a step backward, but I knew that there would be no escape from this latest indignity.

Johnson reached down and clipped it to my collar. Both sides read: PLEASE DON'T FEED ME.

"This will protect Randolph from himself," Johnson said, handing over a small bag filled with hard purple pellets. "Now, I need your help on this since I can't do it alone. I will be doing everything in my power—giving two hundred fifty-three percent—to get this guy moving, getting him limber, and keeping the garbage out of his gullet, but you're going to be the guy who has to do the job of being the consistent and responsible feeder. Can you do this?"

Harry nodded.

"Good," Johnson said. "That bag is filled with specially formulated high-fiber food pellets. Randolph gets two fist-sized portions of those a day."

"For a total of four a day?"

"For a total of deuce."

"That's it?"

"That's it," Johnson said.

"Is there a reason that they're purple?"

"Organic beet coloring for extra power and fewer calories," Johnson said. "Now, here's the plan. He's going to be going leashless, right?"

"That's what I was thinking. Shouldn't he?"

"By all means," Johnson said. "It'll just up the threat level."

"The threat level?"

"That sign is very sophisticated," Johnson said. "If Randolph gets within five feet of food, it will deliver a high-pitched sound that our friend will find exceedingly unpleasant, and which one of us or other designated members of the crew will know how to rapidly respond to. Calorie reduction is the only way at this point. You and I both know that his condition is critical. Any questions?"

Harry had no questions, and his dog had no means to ask any questions or raise any objections. Two fistfuls a day of purple food product lay ahead. Dreams of the midnight buffet had crumbled.

"Hear about the suicide?" Jock Johnson asked.

Harry nodded.

"It puts a real damper on things," Johnson said. "But you've got to hand it to her husband. I never thought much of him before, but I take my hat off to him. He's going on with the show—doing a full schedule of classes and events—not letting tragedy get in the way of his life. That's the hallmark of a real champion . . . the three f's: firmness, finesse, and focus."

Apparently, appropriateness, decorum, and the ability to be frozen, savaged, or scarred by life's inexplicable cruelties were concepts foreign to Jock Johnson. I suppose the world is easier to manage when it is built around lowering caloric intake and your time in running the mile. I alone would be left with the tragic problem of Kitty Tabasco. Johnson dismissed us with instructions to appear for "intensive PE" at seven the following morning.

Then Harry dismissed me. "Have a ball, fella," he said. "And don't get into any trouble."

I looked up at him plaintively. It was strange to wander off like this on my own, liberated from leash and master.

"Come on," Harry said. "It will be good for you."

Not one to disobey a direct order, I walked off with the pink monstrosity dangling from my neck and the knowledge that my grumbling stomach would only get worse. But I had something larger than myself to worry about now. I had the strange case of Kitty Tabasco. And I knew my first stop.

A DOG IS UNDERSTOOD

———

THE CAPTAIN MAKES AN ANNOUNCEMENT

SEVERAL TELEVISION CELEB-rities were teaching workshops on our first morning at sea. There was the famed dog nutritionist Sarah Farley-Knapp, running a standing-room-only presentation called Fancy Snacks for Finicky Feeders; the monks—or at least two of them; the third was still said to be fasting and praying in their stateroom—were hosting a specialized "spiritual" intervention for hyperactive dogs called Bridging the Gap: Soul Talk Between Your Pet and You; and, finally, there was Milton Tabasco, the Dog Mutterer.

He was my target.

While Ivan had spoken disparagingly about my weight and Jock Johnson had first tried to dope me and then outlined ways to starve and exercise-torture me, Yours Truly had continued to puzzle over Kitty Tabasco's demise.

Yes, Ivan had reported an eyewitness to Kitty's plunge, but the woman, whoever she was, sounded unreliable. Why would a person wait to report such an emergency? Perhaps the answer lay in drunkenness, but still... And then there was the question of Milton Tabasco's scent. As precise as my nose is and as definite as scents can be, they are not a precise, predictive indicator of future behavior. Scents speak of emotions and intentions, but never in an A-equals-B sort of way.

To clarify: I'm not a mind reader, though some dogs might be. Certainly the cases involving canines who seem to have an uncanny ability to know exactly when their owners are coming home deserve scientific investigation. But those are intuitions that are beyond me— much the way that a human might have heard of extraordinary psychic abilities in other humans but never experienced them himself.

It's important for our purposes, though, that I state my olfactory ability as plainly as I can. My sense of smell, as wondrous as it may be, is still only a standard physical sense. What I had smelled on Tabasco was both his character—ruthlessly ambitious—and a certain intentionality, a kind of murderous conviction that I assumed must have been building for a long time. But many convictions are never acted upon, and many bad characters keep the extent of their evil unknown by taking the safe road.

That said, I had never thought that Kitty would have taken her own life—her scent was one of sadness and heartbreak, not self-annihilation. I doubted her suicide and suspected her husband, whom I found, less than six hours after the event, at work.

The Dog Mutterer, swamped by popular demand, was holding his class on the Poop Deck and projecting his voice through a megaphone against a stiff wind blowing sternward. That this was the scene of his wife's death seemed to have no effect on him. Tabasco skipped through the crowd smiling and shouting his trademarked nonsense language.

Dozens of dogs and their owners had clustered around him and he was screaming for them to spread out, pointing at where he wanted each pair and telling them not to get offended by his language because he was going to be using the uncensored Tourette's technique that couldn't make it unbleeped onto television.

When he had gotten everyone settled, his expression changed into a pained and mournful one. He narrowed his eyes, furrowed his brow, and lowered his voice.

"Many of you might think that it is strange that I am holding this class in light of what happened here on this very spot last night."

A few heads bobbed. The Dog Mutterer began to tear, and his voice thickened. I moved in closer to detect his scent and learn what it might tell me about his genuine emotions.

"I'm speaking of Kitty Tabasco. My wife, my faithful companion, my business partner, my friend, my muse, the woman who inspired me, the woman who believed in my trademarked dog-training techniques when the whole world thought I was crazy, the woman who made me who I am today. I lost that Kitty last night when she took her own life and..."

The tears began to bulge.

"...and..."

They began to trickle down the Dog Mutterer's cheeks.

"...and..."

Tabasco wiped them away with the hand holding the megaphone. Then he paused, drew breath, and began again.

"...and that's why I'm standing here now. Because she would want me to be standing before you right now, going on against the odds. I can almost see Kitty here at this very moment cheering me on."

I found it hard to believe that the ghost of a suicidal Kitty Tabasco would be motivated to cheer Milton on, so I stepped over a woman sitting on the deck with her pointer to get closer to his scent. Suddenly I was enveloped in it. Milton, it seemed, didn't believe this, either.

There was nothing in his scent that supported the tears, the pained expression, and the stuttering and husky heartbroken voice. There was no difference between the scent of Tabasco at the dining table or in the lounge with the monk and this Tabasco. No difference at all.

The potent, dangerous ambition was there, as was the concealing charm. Had you blindfolded me and asked me to describe what the bearer of these scents resembled, I would have said that all you'd see on the surface was a smile and welcoming eyes; maybe if you were a very astute visual observer, you might have noticed a kind of physical energy in his carriage or certain movements that suggested the ambition. But I would have never guessed this mask of sorrow.

"Kitty was not always a gentle woman. As you know from my show, she could be tough and incredibly demanding when things weren't done right. Sometimes she rubbed people the wrong way—and what a mouth! You think my mouth is bad..."

There was muted, respectful laughter from the crowd at this point, recognizing the tragedy while acknowledging the momentary bright sliver in the dark, dark cloud.

"But in all seriousness, she was not gentle for a very good reason. She could be demanding for a purpose. You see, Kitty does—did—things right, and she loved dogs more than life itself. She knew that dogs, our closest animal friends on this planet, on this whole screwed-up planet, deserved the best. She fought for that and—you know what?—people didn't always like hearing the truth. They didn't like to hear that if their dogs misbehaved it wasn't their dogs' fault, it was a failure of communication. They didn't like her belief that dogs are beings worthy of respect and aren't just accessories. I want you all to be the first to know that I am establishing a scholarship in her name for a select person to study animal behavior at a university of their choice *and* a foundation to ensure that man–dog relations will continue to improve around the world so that her legacy will live on long after today."

There was general applause. And after flashing his smile in every direction and wiping the sun-sparkling tear traces from his eyes, he bellowed enthusiastically into the megaphone: "Now enough of this sadness! Let's start communicating with our pets!"

Yours Truly had learned what he wanted and began to back away. Anywhere, I suspected, would be better than being assaulted by Milton Tabasco screaming meaningless strings of words into a megaphone. I could visit the monks. When I had passed their presentation on my way to the Poop Deck, I noticed that they had several bottles of their award-winning orange schnapps at the ready. They were known for employing it as a secret weapon against hyperactive dogs. This would be amusing, as would the overly eager celebrity chef and her delectables (I would not get too close lest I set off the big pink spongy monstrosity hanging from my neck). Even merely to wander around the ship unencumbered for a while and think upon what I had learned would be pleasant. Yes, anything other than being screamed at by a possibly murderous maniac with a megaphone.

But it was not to be. Milton Tabasco had spotted me and he needed a straight dog.

"Folks, see this guy getting ready to leave ... He's

backing right the hell up. Why? Because I'm not doing my job."

Then he impersonated the kind of animal I decidedly wasn't.

"I'm out of here, Dog Mutterer," Tabasco imagined me thinking. "Your TV show *looks* impressive, how you talk to all those dogs and stuff, but I'm not buyin' it. I've got to go find me some food."

People stared at the Labrador with the generous belly and the pink spongy around his neck and laughed.

"That's what this guy is saying. And you know what? He's totally, four hundred and fifty-six and a half percent right. They *can* do all sorts of things on TV and make things look real good when they're totally bogus."

Tabasco read my sign aloud to the crowd.

"Please Don't Feed Me," he screamed into the megaphone. "Don't worry, buddy, we won't. We're not about pet abuse around here."

This was far from obvious.

"Okay, buddy, you're gonna be my partner today and I'm gonna show you exactly how real my methods are. I'm gonna convince you that I really can talk to animals. Sound like a plan, folks?"

The crowd applauded wildly and some began to repeat the words on my sign as if it were uproariously funny: *Don't Feed Me! Don't Feed Me!*

Tabasco held up his hand to silence them.

"Folks, let's start Muttering!"

I began to walk away.

"Not so fast, buddy," Tabasco said. "You're my partner, remember? The people need a model before they try it themselves."

He fired a volley of his potent dog-speak at me. "Jelly bean...master craftsman...fart sandwich..."

It had the same effect on me as it had in the lounge the previous day. I found myself sitting, shaking my paw, and, despite my best efforts to resist, rolling over onto my back and presenting my belly to the whole world. And then I was back on my paws.

"Garbanzo...caterpillar...plate tectonics...mush bucket," Tabasco said.

I bowed.

This power to control me was too strange for my liking, and I decided that I had had enough. So I barked (I can count the number of times in my post-puppy life that I have used this crude vocal tool).

"So you've had enough, have you?" Tabasco asked. That the Dog Mutterer could have deduced my frustrations from my barking was not surprising. I'm not sure what got into me, but I decided to bark some more and this time I was listing my complaints in my head as I did. This is when things grew stranger.

"And you think that I have no right to hypnotize you—that's what you think I'm doing?—and that you have been humiliated because you never give your paw to anyone and the belly display was well beneath your dignity..."

The words that came out of Tabasco's mouth

tracked Yours Truly's thoughts. The Dog Mutterer looked genuinely perplexed by what he was saying. He turned to the crowd.

"A pretty sophisticated dog, hey, folks?"

As this was happening I told myself it wasn't happening. After being as isolated from humans as I have been for all of my life, the possibility that Tabasco could actually understand me was bracing. I decided to continue the experiment.

"And you want to insist that that pink spongy sign around your neck was none of your doing and you don't believe that you are as obese as everyone says (you have an unusually wide rib cage) nor do you think—given the data that are available—that a little extra weight is detrimental to canine life expectancy. Far more detrimental is the lack of joy that comes from not partaking in the delectables on offer, especially those to be found at the midnight buffet..."

Tabasco was out of breath as if just barely keeping pace with my verbal download. He seemed surprised and out of sorts and sought the support of the crowd again.

"I'm not kidding you, folks, this guy really is saying all of this. I haven't seen anything like it. If he keeps it up, I'm gonna sell him to the Russians, I hear they're still looking for bright dogs for their space program."

Was this a compliment or a veiled threat? Surely the prospect of being whisked away to a Siberian training camp in anticipation of being rocketed into orbit was not for real. In any case, I believed they used monkeys or wombats for these missions. Still, Tabasco's growing interest in Yours Truly should have given me pause. It did not. I continued to bark and Tabasco continued to translate. Just as he had exerted hypnotic control over me, I seemed to have a similar influence over him. What I thought as I barked came out as words for Tabasco. It was intoxicating. I had chills up and down my spine and gave myself a full-body shake to maintain my equilibrium.

"And you have a problem with the gross commercialization of our world especially as it pertains to the arts and dogs. Take dogs, for example. No human really knows what's going on in their heads—you can say that again, buddy!—and yet all of human society is designed around the behavioralist assumption that dogs and all other animals don't have consciousness. Science, which is used to explore all kinds of phenomena, has not been harnessed to discover the hidden things in this world like animal consciousness. Simply because an animal can't express itself in words, appear to behave practically or with so-called sense (a human construct after all), and can't dominate the physical world as humans have done—then it's inferior. I have long wondered if the Neanderthals, which humans might have slaughtered or driven to extinction in some other way, were not actually peaceful and refined philosophers, the truly enlightened of the two species, who refused to embrace violence even if it meant their own extinction."

Tabasco shook his head. Members of the crowd were beginning to look at one another as if they were wondering whether Tabasco was having a breakdown.

I decided to deliver one more volley.

"And why did I kill my . . ."

Tabasco pushed the alarm button on the megaphone. My ears and the ears of every dog within one hundred feet seemed to catch fire. The sound was excruciating. Dogs howled and whined. I stopped barking.

"Sorry about that, folks. Pushed the wrong button," Tabasco said, turning off the alarm. The Dog Mutterer looked shaken. The robust, ruddy cheeks were pale and, more telling, a distinct scent of fear and bewilderment exuded from him now. In between glances up at the crowd, he delivered me what can only be described as a dangerous look.

I had clearly amazed him, but whatever amazement he felt in finding an articulate and highly intelligent dog in his morning workshop was overshadowed by my last sentence, which he only partially repeated. In full, it was: "And why did I kill my wife by throwing her off the Poop Deck in the middle of the night."

But Tabasco was a professional, and an instant later he had gathered himself and gone on with the show.

"Folks, now it's your turn," he said. "If you turn to page two of the pamphlet that Charlotte, my assistant, handed out at the beginning of the session, you'll see how you deliver the *sit* command in Dog-Mutterer-speak."

In an instant the Poop Deck was alive with obscenities.

"That's the way," the Mutterer encouraged.

Tabasco bent down in front of me, switched off the megaphone, and laid it on the deck. He put one hand on the side of my head and scratched my ear with the other. Despite my intense dislike of Tabasco, he was a very good ear scratcher and this is, regrettably, paralyzing for my kind.

"So what are we going to do with you?" Tabasco said. "The first intelligent dog I meet and he accuses me of murdering my wife. How about that? Well, fella, let me tell you, you've got it wrong, and even if you got it right I'm the only one who can understand you."

Tabasco began to twist my ear around his fingers and pull ever so slightly.

"You goddamn know it all. The world isn't black and white. Relationships aren't simple things. There's no justice inside a marriage. No one on the outside of any situation ever knows what it's like to be on the inside. Especially a dog."

He pulled a little harder so that I was aware of the potential for even greater pain.

"I feel sorry for you," Tabasco said. "All that knowledge, all that thinking ability trapped inside your skull and no one to share it with. You're one sorry piece of work. No wonder you stuff yourself silly. No one to confide in. No one to share this life with. That's sad. And now you think you've got this little secret, which, by the way, you're all wrong about, and you're just dying to share it with somebody. But there's nobody to share it with except me, the one person on the planet you shouldn't."

Tabasco released his grip. "Get lost, pal," he said. "I've got a class to teach."

Sandbagged by this bizarre soliloquy, I began to walk away.

"Don't feed yourself to death," Tabasco called after me. "And be careful on deck. Don't get washed overboard. I hear we're in for nasty weather."

Stunned, I wandered and weaved through humans and dogs around Deck 13 and into the interior of the ship. I have had moments in my life when people have treated me as if I understood their words (it's a common enough occurrence for most dogs to become the confidant of last resort to an army of sad sacks). But never had I engaged in an actual conversation with a human and then been treated to a lecture filled with threats.

Why suggest imminent harm to Yours Truly if he was certain I could not communicate with anyone else? And why the melodramatic reference to nasty weather, as if my uncertain future needed any more hyperbole? My first communication with a human and it had ended dismally.

As it turned out, the reference was not melodramatic at all. Tabasco possessed advance knowledge. With the rise and fall of a boatswain's whistle all the flat-screen televisions interrupted the now permanently featured Sedadog™ video for an announcement from Captain Bostitch.

"Ladies and gentlemen," said Captain Bostitch. He was dressed in all white, and the brim of his starched hat gleamed in the bright light of the bridge where he stood with his hand draped over an antique wooden wheel in what was otherwise a perfectly modernized command, blinking with colorful readouts and bedecked with buttons.

"Ladies and gentlemen, your attention," he repeated. His tone tended toward the grave, but I detected a manic joy just beneath the surface. "We have been informed by the North Atlantic Weather Bureau that a tropical depression has developed off the coast of the Leeward Islands and is moving toward us. As you know, it is unusual for such a storm to develop so early in the season, but the sea—like a woman, especially a French woman—is unpredictable and we must all pay the price for this fact. While I am anticipating trouble from this storm and a necessary disruption of some of the shipboard frivolities and possibly the loss of life, you can be assured that this ship and your captain are prepared for, even eagerly awaiting, any kind of horror that the sea can throw at us—and there are many. For your edification, this meteorological phenomenon, tentatively called Tropical Depression Reginald, will undergo a name change if it becomes a tropical storm. In which eventuality, since the North Atlantic Weather Bureau is currently auctioning branding rights to the highest corporate bidder, the storm will be known as Tropical Storm Sedadog™. If it becomes a hurricane, then we will be battered and savaged by Hurricane Sedadog Extra™. Foolhardy that, since even a marketing novice will tell you to avoid connecting a negative experience with your product. But I have no further comment regarding suspect new methods for creating buzz. Mine is just to do or die not to reason why. Though if they take to naming storms after celebrities or blockbuster movies, I shall stand my ground, draw a line in the sand, sir, you may be assured. And please also note that smoking is not permitted in the panoramic Nordic Sun Lounge on Deck Sixteen. Also, the traditional Scandinavian Treasure Hunt will commence promptly at fourteen hundred hours. Thank you and, remember, keep one hand for the rigging."

The absurd but unsettling Bostitch disappeared with another boatswain whistle, leaving the passengers around me chattering about what it all meant and whether our safety was really threatened.

"I wish we had a straight-shooting American captain," someone said. "Not this eccentric British guy."

"It ain't going to be nothing but a little wind and rain," someone else declared.

I spied the compulsive quilters in a corner responding to the announcement by quilting more furiously. The college coeds apparently just out of bed were in search of mimosas and brunch.

Yours Truly needed a place to gather himself before he, too, began gobbling down Sedadog™ and, so benumbed, began enjoying popular novelists and watching light move.

THE PASSAGEWAY I FINALLY stumbled upon was damp and smelled of old books and periodicals. A heavenly scent for this Labrador bibliophile.

Wandering for what seemed like hours, I had passed invisible through clouds of dog enthusiasts and their dogs educating themselves at the hands of canine masters, tequila-drinking crowds wearing baseball caps and listening to a song about a wastrel searching for saltshakers in the tropics, several adventurous types climbing the rock wall, people shooting skeet off the rear of the ship, and even a lecture on the dangers of buttock enhancement surgery delivered by a woman with a dangerously enhanced left buttock and a shrunken right one.

But here I was detecting comforting literacy and reflection. The *Nordic Bliss* might have been replete with high-volume, garish entertainments, but at least it was not without a library.

To tell the truth, I had still not gained my sea legs

and had also underestimated the importance of routine, habit, and home in my mental well-being. Tabasco had stung me by reminding me of my solitude and how my stone face and muteness made me a prisoner in the human world. But he was wrong in that books have always provided me with a bridge off that island.

The ship's library was about the size of our cozy abode in Manhattan and was lined with books from all periods and genres. A pleasantly plump middle-aged woman sat behind a desk doing a crossword, an emerald-green sweater draped over her shoulders against the chill from an air-conditioning duct above her head.

As I entered she looked at me for a moment, smiled, and then continued with her crossword.

"You're my first visitor all day," she said. "Make yourself at home."

This seemed a sad testament to human literacy (or at least interest in the written word), but I was profoundly happy to find a large, plush rug on which to lie and even happier to see that someone had left an open book on the edge of this rug. It was an illustrated history of the castles and vineyards of the Rhine Valley. I would discreetly turn the pages and, lost in a tour of the continent, leave Tabasco and the impending tropical depression/storm/hurricane far behind.

And as frequently happened when I read, my mind calmed sufficiently and I cleared room to think. When I emerged after an escapist half hour in the Rhine Valley, I was ready to consider my options.

Tabasco, I concluded, would not kill me—at least not unless I made myself a nuisance. He might not have been a reasonable man—and why should he be, since he possessed a gift that wasn't supposed to exist?—but I hadn't detected that scent, a mixture of wild cherry, licorice, and kerosene, that marks lunatics. And if he was reasonable, and he must have been reasonable enough to have built a dog-training, merchandising empire, then he would calm down and eventually conclude that I posed no threat to him. He might even seek me out to apologize.

After I had gotten my immediate fear out of the way, I began to think of his exact words. It was strange that he had suggested that he might be innocent of his wife's death and then soon after seemed to contradict himself by justifying: *Relationships aren't simple things. There's no justice inside a marriage.* Moreover, my nose had begun to confuse me because as he had said these things, I had picked up both possibilities: that Tabasco both had and had not killed Kitty. None of this made very much sense. Still, whether or not he had disposed of his wife on the high seas, the Dog Mutterer was likely one of a handful of television personalities to actually deserve the public adulation he had received.

It was also clear that unlike past adventures, I was in the unusual position of being able to investigate without having to rely on the unpredictable travel habits of my owner. This time I was aboard the equivalent of an

English Country House Mystery, the kind of environment immortalized by Dame Agatha Christie. There was no escape for either murderer or detective, and the facts of the case would be discoverable if only I had the ability to do so. Ah, but was I getting ahead of myself? After all, no one except for me thought there had been a murder, and even I wasn't completely certain now.

What I could do was observe. The pink spongy would make it difficult for me to remain inconspicuous, but perhaps I didn't need to remain inconspicuous. Why not taunt Tabasco with my presence? Follow him about above- and belowdecks. Track his every move. I could always run away (or at least briskly walk).

And then there was the question of the lone witness to Kitty's plunge. If Tabasco were lying and he had killed Kitty, then this woman was also lying and I would need to find her—but how on a ship with fifteen hundred passengers? I would need to enlist someone's help or find some other way of having her come to me. Of course, if I kept close to Tabasco and she was his accomplice—perhaps even a lover—then surely they would meet at some point and I would witness this. But what good would it do unless I overheard what they were saying—unlikely, since I had already decided to keep a safe distance lest Tabasco pick me up and heave me over the side of the ship. Far better would be to locate this woman and then have someone else question her while I took a lie-detecting snout sample.

I needed Harry's help. Fortunately, there was the

Internet. Perhaps I could communicate with him this way. I noticed a station tucked away in one corner of the library. Unfortunately, I doubted whether Harry would be checking his e-mail for the duration of our journey. But just as I thought I would have to find another way, a passenger arrived and asked the librarian about something called the Virtual Telegram service. The librarian proceeded to describe the answer to my problems. The Virtual Telegram service was available from any of the digital kiosks around the ship and allowed a passenger to send a message to any other passenger's room. The message would be displayed on that passenger's entertainment system. It was the paper-saving answer to shipboard telegrams. Need to change meeting places? Virtual Telegram. Want to eat a meal earlier or later? Virtual Telegram. Want to enlist your owner in a possibly madcap bid to prove the Dog Mutterer has murdered his wife? Virtual Telegram was the way to go.

But the Virtual Telegram would have to wait. At a quarter to one, the librarian rose from her desk and informed me that I must leave because she was shutting for lunch. I stood and stretched into a downward dog.

"You're a sweet old thing, aren't you?"

I did a full-body shake in response and my tail wagged more enthusiastically than I would have liked.

"Very sweet," she said locking the door behind us.

I missed Harry and decided to find him. Even

though the *Nordic Bliss* allowed passengers to eat whenever and as often as they liked—I noticed that the car
salesman from Pasadena had gained an inch around his
already plump waist—the halls and lounges were empty
for lunch as I made my way to the site of the never-end-
ing buffet in the Valhalla Vista, an enormous banquet
hall that dominated the rear half of Deck 14 and commanded sweeping views of the ocean, which at this
hour showed no signs of Captain Bostitch's promised
storm.

The air of Valhalla Vista set my nose to high ecstasy.
I sometimes fear that a reader might think less of me
because of my constant reference to the power of the
olfactory sense, especially as it relates to food. But I can
do nothing about this. If only the reader were him- or
herself aware of how certain senses and impressions—
often just beneath the surface of consciousness—
influence whether a day is considered a good one or a
bad one. Anyone who has lived has felt moments of
sudden inexplicable joy or waves of deep sadness as if
from nowhere. But really, most of these emotions are
from somewhere. They are from stimuli you cannot detect that awaken associations and memories that you
cannot remember.

My nose's ecstasy in encountering the steam tables
piled high with food in Valhalla Vista was the product of
so many scents—all of which I isolated and rejoiced
in—and so many related memories. For the brain, remembering is reliving. The neurons that fired when we

first had the experience, fire again. There were: fried pork dumplings in soy/rice vinegar dipping sauce (how many cold winter nights in Imogen's absence had Harry and I found comfort in them?); spaghetti Bolognese (one of Imogen's specialties; she had labored over the magnificent sauce, taking it from fresh crushed tomato, onion, and garlic to its satiny finish); quiche (ham, cheese, and chives with Harry and Imogen on Sunday mornings at Georgia's Bakery on Broadway and 90th); and, finally, a New York–style cheesecake (this, of course, was something that Harry and Imogen both would return with and always serve me an ample sliver whether or not I employed my eyes' most mournful and deserving gaze).

In near trance and light-headed from lack of food (I had only eaten those meager breakfast treats and was now on a starvation diet), I wandered the hall looking for my owner. There were so many people and so much chaos that I could not find him. Many dogs were eating from plates at their owners' feet. A few were gobbling down treasures from the buffet that their owners had snuck under the table for them, but most were feeding on either run-of-the-mill dried food or those bizarre purple nuggets that were my new diet as well. And then there was the communal water trough along one wall— I had seen others about the ship.

I knew that if I could not find Harry, I should leave promptly lest I be overcome by the fumes from the buffet and do something rash. But I did not leave. The smells had invaded my brain, and I found myself stand-ing in the middle of the floor revisiting the past on a magic carpet of olfactory associations. I stood there frozen with my neurons all afire experiencing the most wonderful time travel but to all appearances just an-other dumb animal standing around without purpose.

Then two things happened. The odd Scandinavian waiter from dinner the night before passed, quickly stooped, and ran his hand down the middle of my back. It was a most pleasant sensation and almost familiar, perhaps, because I was thinking of Imogen and the two experiences melded. Then, just as I was considering this, I saw Milton Tabasco, megaphone still in his hand, march right across my field of vision and alongside the steam tables in the center of the room.

He did not notice me and moved fast, ignoring the vast array of edibles and the roomful of dogs. Tabasco seemed to be looking for someone; when he didn't see whoever it was, he quickened his already rapid pace and made for the exit at the opposite end of the room.

The sight of him awoke me from my reverie. I con-sidered following, but just then a piece of paper fell from his back pocket. Tabasco didn't notice it. I saun-tered over and scooped it up in my jaws. Unfortunately, I did not consider the sensitivity of my pink sponge food alarm to the proximity of the steam tables.

The alarm triggered, and the noise was horrible. The dogs in the room began to howl. I thought my 2.3 pounds of smoothly functioning gray matter would drain from my ears. Then I found myself subjected to an even worse indignity.

Jock Johnson was there. The Pet Wellness Compliance Officer had been eating a healthy diet of fresh greens and low-fat Thousand Island dressing when he saw his desperate case make what he assumed was a raid on the buffet. Johnson sprinted toward me. In an instant, he had lifted me off the floor, hung me upside down, and began to shake vigorously as if he were trying to loose clotted ketchup from the mouth of the bottle.

"Drop it," Johnson shouted. "Drop it."

But I clung to the paper and Johnson continued to shake until I felt even the remnants of my pitiful breakfast might make a reappearance. I was now the center of attention and the pink spongy with its PLEASE DON'T FEED ME jangling about was having the same prejudicial effect on the dog-owning passengers as the Scarlet Letter had on the Salem pious.

"How could they have let him get so out of control?" the owner of a butterfly-weight terrier whispered.

"It's the Labrador breed that's the problem," the anorexic owner of an anorexic poodle replied. "They're lazy by nature and if you don't watch every little morsel, they're in trouble. Pathetic. It's a warning to us all."

Meanwhile I was bounced up and down in the arms of the overzealous Johnson, who was determined to part Tabasco's paper from my jaws. Finally, dizzy and humiliated, I let the paper drop. Johnson placed me back on the floor. My pink sponge alarm stopped ringing. The crowd went back to attacking the buffet.

But Jock Johnson wasn't done with me. He crammed his fingers, one with an enormous fraternity ring on the pinkie, into my mouth in search of the illegal food he was certain was there.

"You meathead," Johnson said. "You swallowed it."

Finally, he gave up and left me with a warning. "I'm not going to be there all the time to save you from yourself. You've got to start respecting your body. Your body is your temple."

After he had walked off, I picked up Tabasco's paper and skulked from the room and away from all the censorious eyes. I found a small niche just outside the Parisian Piano Bar on Deck 11. No one was around and the light was adequate. I nosed open Tabasco's paper.

It was an empty business envelope folded in half. The front had the logo of the Curaçao Electric Utility Bureau in the upper left-hand corner and blacked-out text where the addressee should have been (though I could still make out a *v* or possibly a *u* on the top line and an *o* with the final letter being *m*). The back had pencil scribbles from top to bottom. I don't know what I expected to find. I suppose I wanted something that would give me traction against Tabasco and evidence of his role in Kitty's demise. From the looks of it, this wasn't it. If anything, it was evidence of Tabasco, the businessman, fretting over his operation in a spill of cryptic numbers and phrases: *4.5 million market share (T)*

3.9 million market share (M) manufacturing capacity tripled at half the cost distribution costs significant cross-marketing products deliver big advertising savings nonprofit status equals additional savings

This meant nothing to me, but I didn't want to lose it, so I nosed it into a hiding place between the couch and the wall.

The clock on the wall told me it was three PM and I decided to search for a Virtual Telegram kiosk through which I could alert Harry to the Tabasco situation. Unfortunately, all of the kiosks were located in high-traffic areas and, in any case, were usually occupied. If I could secure a free one, I would only be able to use it briefly, and even then I ran the risk of detection. I decided to return to the library where I hoped I might have better luck and could at least catch up on my sleep.

As I made my way through the corridors, a band of Scandinavian Treasure Hunters—or rather passengers on the Scandinavian Treasure Hunt—raced past me down the hallway clutching miscellaneous booty including jars of lingonberries and sundry *hemslöjd,* traditional Scandinavian crafts like dala horses and ceramic trolls.

The library was open again. I was greeted civilly by its pleasant minder and planned to seize any spare moment when the librarian stepped away so that I could nose out a Virtual Telegram to my owner. In the meantime I would spend the hours until dinner napping and reading discreetly from whatever was now in snout-swiping range. Unfortunately, the tour of the Rhine Valley book had been shelved, and all that remained in reach were industry periodicals including *Commercial Concrete* and *The Small Restaurant Entrepreneur*. I learned more that afternoon about proper mainte-nance techniques for a deep-fryer than a Labrador needs to know and then dreamed of being rolled in flour and dropped into boiling oil by Milton Tabasco. The hours passed and during my conscious moments the librarian never left me alone.

I awoke to a gentle nudge in my ribs and looking up saw Harry smiling down at me, his face burned red from a day asleep on a deck chaise. I delivered a down-ward dog with upward eye contact and a manic tail wag to express my happiness at seeing my owner.

"I've been looking all over the ship for you, Randolph," Harry said. "There's a storm coming."

TROPICAL DEPRESSION REGInald had been promoted to Tropical Storm Sedadog™ and the *Nordic Bliss,* somewhere off Cape Hatteras and sailing along the cusp of the Bermuda Triangle, had begun to heave and roll. Harry took me on deck. The sea rose and fell in massive swells. The air had become warm and humid. A wall of clouds that looked as dark and heavy as concrete stretched from the horizon to far above our heads like an enormous lid that was about to close. Wind whined through the railings and punched at the ship in sudden gusts. The Scandinavians stacked the chairs, tied down everything loose, and checked the lifeboats. A discarded canary-yellow sheet, one of the cruise director's cherished activities schedules, skittered across the deck and overboard into the sea.

With no passengers about, it was eerie standing outside. I gave myself a shake and looked up at Harry to encourage him to take us into dinner. Even if all that awaited were two fistfuls of purple food product, it would be bright and convivial inside. I had also seen an announcement for a theatrical revue at eight that night in the Broadway-style theater. I had never seen a live performance, having lived in contented constraint in our Manhattan apartment.

But instead Harry leaned on the railing and looked out to sea. I stood beside him, occasionally having to check my balance with an extended paw whenever the ship made a heavy roll.

"He told me six o'clock," Harry said, and I knew then that he was waiting for someone. I expected that in a moment Ivan Manners or Jackson Temple would appear. I was relieved that it was not a "she" since the only she likely would have been the persistent Zest Kilpatrick, whom I suspected must have been going stir crazy aboard a ship with only human interest stories to film and would be more eager than ever to stake amorous claim to my owner.

Ten minutes must have passed during which I became lost in watching the sea. Suddenly I was awakened.

"Harry," a man with a thick Australian accent said as he passed behind us. "Don't turn around. Count to ten and then follow me."

It was Blinko Patterson, the guardian of Imogen's fortune, who among other things had saved my life during my adventures in the midnight kitchen of a United Nations chef determined to turn me into a culinary delicacy. Blinko Patterson had become our guide and source of insight into the dark forces that our mistress faced and the reasons for her disappearance from our lives.

The fortune was a vast uranium deposit in Australia. Imogen was set to inherit it if she reached thirty and was deemed sane by the executor of the estate. This executor happened to be Blinko, a lawyer and friend of Imogen's grandfather. Her grandfather had been a demanding and unreasonable man whom my mistress had never met and who was haunted by the prospect that his granddaughter heir would be a lunatic like his own daughter, whom his fortune had skipped.

This complicated family soup was made more complex by the fact that an energy-hungry world wanted to take Imogen's claim away from her before she had even received it. Agents of every nationality seemed intent on doing this by the most Machiavellian and bloodthirsty of means. For his part, as much as he wanted to fight this danger and injustice, Blinko could not become too involved: The terms of the trust dictated that he remain on the sidelines.

Harry counted to ten and then followed the enormous Australian toward the front of the ship. We climbed one flight of stairs and then another until finally we had arrived at a dead end, a small open space on which no one could spy on us unseen.

Blinko stopped at the far railing and turned around. He was wearing a storm coat that made him seem even larger.

"Well, here we are," Blinko said.

"It's good to see you," Harry said.

"You too, mate."

"It makes it more real," my owner said. "As if she's actually going to be there waiting when we arrive."

"I reckon it's real enough," Blinko said. "The whole thing'll be sorted . . . if you don't lose your head and don't forget that she is still being hunted. If I tracked you down, then they can track you down. Not to sound melodramatic, but there are enemies all around you. Can you trust that wealthy blighter with the tree sloth?"

"Jackson?" Harry asked. "With my life."

"How about that fat bloke with the lorikeet?"

"Ivan," Harry said. "I don't tell Ivan anything."

"Good. What a bloody whinger," Blinko said. Then he dropped his voice. "And that fiery duck with the red hair?"

"Zest," Harry said. "I wouldn't worry about her."

"I worry about any journo with a camera and I especially worry about that woman. She is interested in you, and she is too much of a professional not to connect some of the facts into a story."

"This doesn't sound like you, Blinko. Where's the old confidence?" Harry asked.

"It's there, mate, it's just tempered by a reality you don't comprehend."

"But we're so close to finding her and ending this," Harry said. "And no one could be following me now. I mean it's so unlikely. You only did because you knew that Imogen would keep on running and you were watching me."

"Just don't get your hopes up and let your guard down, Harry," Blinko said. "In this life it's better to have low expectations and a sense of imminent failure than high expectations and a certainty of success."

Then he turned his attention to me. "And how are you doing, mate? Keeping close watch over the young master? I hope so. Mark my words, you'll be needed."

This last comment reminded me that Blinko had always seemed to detect strengths and hidden attributes in Yours Truly that others missed. His words encouraged but also sobered me, as if something was expected in an almost epic way far beyond the usual demands placed upon a pet.

The concrete-heavy clouds and the disappearing sun had squeezed all the light from the sky. I was aware only of the seething invisible ocean beyond the railing as you might be of something venomous moving in the dark.

Blinko began to edge away from us.

"Wait," Harry said. "You wanted to tell me something, but you haven't. What is it?"

Blinko paused and looked down at the deck.

"You know I've been in a funny position when it comes to you and Imogen both from the beginning, and I don't mean the legal arrangements," Blinko said. "I was in love once, too. Not so much drama as you pair, but a mate-for-life gambit. I think you know what I mean . . . that if it wasn't her, it wasn't to be anyone else."

Harry nodded.

"And then one day there was an accident. I was far away. They told me she had been hurt. When I arrived she was dead and had been dead before they told me about the accident, dead when they told me she was hurt, dead as I drove there thinking she wasn't dead."

"I'm sorry," Harry said.

"I reckon that's why I'm here," Blinko said. "There's honor, but there's also self-interest, wanting to see it all made right."

Harry put his hand on Blinko's shoulder. "So what is it?" he asked.

"Nothing definite," Blinko said. "I tapped a few sources in New York. There could be several people already on the ground in Curaçao looking for her as we speak."

Harry laughed. "That's crazy," my owner said. "No one could possibly know."

"Perhaps," Blinko said. "But a few very good brains could have calculated the odds of Imogen's survival in the harbor that night, the odds of you taking this cruise without a purpose, and analyzing all the places that she had been known to visit or have some connection to. If they're down in Curaçao, there is nothing we can do. It is already over."

"I can't think that," Harry said. "I've been opened up to possibility and shut right down again too many times in the last year and a half. She's alive and I'm going to find her. At the end of this story, Imogen's sitting on a beach waiting for me."

"Rightio," Blinko said. "That's the way it should be. It was pointless for me to make you a party to my worries. I'll have your back in any case."

"If there are people shadowing me, any idea who they might be?"

"Not a bloody clue. My guess is they'll be the most conspicuous characters on this ship, all Hawaiian shirts, cameras with flashbulbs, and loud obvious talk about American hometowns that is completely bogus," Blinko said. "But don't fret, they can only do one thing: try to follow you to Imogen. If they kill you, you're worthless to them."

When Blinko left us, we went back inside the ship. The violent motion of the *Nordic Bliss* had been less apparent in the open air, but inside, the corridors rose and fell, walls tilted, and passengers staggered. The Scandinavians were busy rolling out vast tracts of brown-colored paper against inevitable upchuck, and people were already beginning to miss meals and entertainment and stick to their rooms.

But sticking to our room was not something that interested Harry this evening. He was restless, and the rivets above the bed and the pipe across the ceiling were creaking louder than ever. After feeding me my two fistfuls of purple food stuff, which only barely calmed the ferocious rumblings in the belly, Harry and I struck out in search of entertainment.

We stopped in at Jackson's suite—which comprised three rooms, one with a most un-Jacksonian hot tub, and a balcony—but he and Marlin, his potted palm brought safely inside, were staying put. Jackson was preparing his shipboard lecture on Rubens, titled A Spy in the House of Art. It was based on an intentionally provocative thesis, which he himself didn't believe, positing that the great Dutch artist had only painted as a cover for his espionage activities for the powers of Europe. While Jackson composed, Marlin was doing the difficult work of adjustment to shipboard life, made all the harder because of a tree sloth's glacial reflexes and the continued swaying of his palm tree. Marlin was subdued and uncommunicative, and although I considered consulting him on the Tabasco matter, I decided that it would have to wait until calmer seas.

"I'm expecting several critics in the audience," Jackson said after he had delivered the essence of his lecture to Harry. "I've just learned that five art history departments are aboard—all of them sworn enemies. I won't be surprised if we come to blows. I am bringing my cane-sword."

When we left Jackson's, Harry told me that I was free to roam again. But after our sobering encounter with Blinko and my concerns about the Tabasco situation, I had no desire to be parted from Harry that evening and stuck close by his side. As we wandered from one brown-papered venue to another—almost all of them empty of passengers—I began to lose hope about attending the Broadway revue. Fortunately we passed the doors of the Lyceum Theater just after the show had started. Sensing that Harry was looking for a place to settle, I took the initiative and walked straight in. Harry followed, and I hopped into a seat.

"You're a funny one," my owner said.

The theater, a vast art deco cavern with crimson-and-gold walls, was empty except for us and a small group clustered in the first row who had to crane their necks up at the performers. The curtains heaved and the stage pitched. At first the performers sang their numbers with explosive smiles as if the house were packed and fans hanging from the rafters. There was a tribute to Irving Berlin done by men in tuxedos circling the stage on roller skates singing "Blue Skies" and "You're in the Army Now, Mr. Jones." Chorus girls in silver dresses joined the men in tuxedos to sing a pastiche of songs extolling Broadway. By this point the men had wisely removed their roller skates after one of them had skated off unscripted into the wings with a slapstick crash.

Next came the great love songs. During "The Surrey with the Fringe on Top," the actress being serenaded about the glories of an up-to-date horse-drawn carriage with isinglass curtains began to drowse off perhaps due to an excess of Dramamine and had to be nudged by her suitor before being replaced mid-serenade by another actress who looked more attentive. Worse lay ahead. During "Some Enchanted Evening," one of the people in the front row bent forward and threw up with Krakatoan force, prompting a chain reaction and an exodus of the entire group from the theater and the flight of a second actress in a duet from the stage.

"This is a horror show," Harry said. My owner, however, was referring more to his own deteriorating condition than the mixed performances onstage. The theater was long enough so that sitting at the back, you became aware of the seesawing of the ship through the waves as you watched the stage rise above you and then fall. Harry had previously complained of dizziness and an upset stomach, and the theater's motion had clearly worsened things. He dropped his head into his hands and began to groan.

Just as the Broadway revue seemed about to collapse—the curtain had dropped mid–Enchanted Evening—the music changed and a phantom voice from offstage—clearly pre-recorded—asked the audience to "give a warm welcome" to the "legendary" jazz and blues singer Vicki LaBoom, a native of Curaçao and a veteran of nightclubs around the world who would be performing in the Parisian Piano Bar for the rest of the week, but who had "kindly agreed" to share her talents with the Broadway revue.

The curtain rose. An enormous black woman advanced toward the edge of the stage, trailed by a spotlight. She wore a satiny purple dress, a string of pearls each not much smaller than those floats that separate lanes in a swimming pool, and a mane of hair that crowned a dramatically made-up face with sparkling eyelashes and great rouged cheeks that told the world *I don't care what you think*. She gripped the microphone as if it were a royal scepter. Here was a theatrical presence that commanded even an empty theater to sit up and be enthralled—a theatrical force that reminded us what stages were built for and made anything that wasn't on the stage, wasn't singing or dancing or making art, somehow pale and unreal. This was talent, drive, charm, and outsized humanity. This was confidence. Before Vicki LaBoom had even opened her mouth to say or sing a word, a certain Labrador not inclined to being a fan of living greats had become a fan of this one.

She was not similarly impressed.

"I've heard about empty houses, but, honey, this is ridiculous," Ms. LaBoom boomed. "We've got one guy in the back who's about to lose it all over the floor and his goddamn dog."

The goddamn dog felt terrible for the grande dame. His owner, as if getting the go-ahead from the singing great, doubled over and heaved on the floor while attempting a one-handed clap for LaBoom on the back of the seat in front of him. I have often been impressed by the courage and wherewithal of the entertainer in the face of hostile or indifferent crowds, but this reception would have broken the best of them. Vicki LaBoom, though an Olympian of the blues and jazz circuit, asked for a chair. When one arrived she sat heavily down in it.

This demanded action so I hurried to the front of the theater, taking a place in the first row.

Vicki LaBoom looked down at me looking up at her. I tried hard to communicate my respect for her through my eyes, my only bridge off my solitary island of consciousness, and somehow something reached her.

"It's hard, sugar," Vicki LaBoom lamented, flicking her fingers through her magnificent hair. "It's hard for you. It's hard for me. It's hard for him."

LaBoom pointed at Harry in the back row who, head down, responded with another great heave. The singer then described a wide circle with her microphone.

"It's hard for the actors and actresses slip-sliding all over this here stage and the people coming on this ship expecting holiday time but getting sick time instead. It's hard for the world, because life is always promising to be fair and then provin' it's not. Well, baby, the storm can keep on blowin', but inside it's safe and warm. Inside we have an antidote. Inside we have the blues and the blues will make everything all right. And we've got Vicki LaBoom singin' them just for you."

And, unbelievable as this may sound and as justified as LaBoom would have been to stalk off the stage and drown her sorrows in orange schnapps, she instead chose to serenade a Labrador retriever sitting in the front row of an empty, storm-tossed theater in the middle of the Atlantic.

She began, appropriately enough, with Billie Holiday's classic "Lady Sings the Blues," but as she waxed and wended her way through one blues standard after another her choices grew lighter until finally we came to "Sunny Side of the Street." The chair had been abandoned, LaBoom was on her feet, billowing across the stage and filling the entire theater with light and joy. I would have danced, but my restrained *Foliage-Finder* nature and my overly cerebral tendencies prevented it. There is nothing sillier than a prancing dog. But inside I moved. Beneath my stone face and my unresponsive body (even my tail was stuck motionless jammed in the seat), I was becoming the music while she sang and my spirit was following each note and phrase to whatever heights or depths it led. Anyone who has ever watched an animal transfixed by something should leave room for this: That in the absence of the voice and gesture needed to express delight and comprehension, it is just possible that there lies a depth of feeling and understanding made sharper by an inability to express it, and refined by its lingering with us longer in solitude.

"Sunny Side of the Street" was LaBoom's finale. She, too, had been somewhere else while she sang, perhaps someone else, and now returned to the grim reality of an empty house and a single nauseous human listener.

Harry, no longer hunched over and heaving onto the floor, clapped weakly.

"Thank you, honey," Vicki LaBoom said. "Now get your sorry ass to bed."

Then she looked down at me. "I'll see you around sometime," LaBoom said.

She stepped backward, the curtain dropped in front of her, and the houselights rose.

I sauntered back to Harry.

"I'm happy that you enjoyed yourself," he said and staggered out into the corridor where he was sick once more.

I WATCHED THE SHIP'S nautical information channel throughout the night as the *Nordic Bliss* battled southward through the tropical storm. We had slowed to a crawl, and the video from the bridge revealed nothing but driving rain and spume drift. Harry was miserable, but he was not the only one in our neighborhood. The coeds had tried to drink their way through the storm and were now paying the price. The virtuous were also being punished. At three AM one of the quilters was rushed to the ship's infirmary groaning loudly, but having the presence of mind to remind one of her nurses not to forget her "Quaint Rabbit in the Teacup" border pattern.

I slept in snatches. At four AM a sound like a motor being revved jarred me from a dream just as Vicki LaBoom had gone into the refrain for "Summertime" after delivering a heaping platter of buffet delectables.

The bolts and steam pipe in our cabin were screeching ever louder, and I had the terrifying sense that we were inside a small tin box that was about to be crushed. The motor sound rose to a fierce pitch and then died again. This was repeated several times. The alarm bells rang. Scandinavians ran up and down the hallways, and the watertight doors slid shut.

Soon the boatswain's whistle was heard and Captain Bostitch's image floated across our television screen. This time the camera rolled for a while before he spoke, and captured him stomping around the bridge, bellowing orders to a single computer technician and finally staring out the tar-black windshield with a fierce man-defying-nature scowl.

He was clearly enjoying himself.

"Ladies and gentlemen, as you are no doubt aware, Tropical Depression Reginald was yesterday upgraded and name-changed to Tropical Storm Sedadog™. This storm is a bit of a bastard and seems to be following my every course correction. If we steered due east I am confident that we would sail beyond the storm; however, that would lead us into the Bermuda Triangle and for the time being I have decided to keep the *Nordic Bliss* out of that nasty patch of woods. As any experienced mariner will tell you, the triangle eats men alive and then enjoys seconds.

"Of course, if we are not clear of the weather by sixteen hundred hours, I will sail directly into the triangle lest bad weather interfere with the celebrity barbecue cook-off and the canine quarter-final wall-climbing event. Also, it has come to my attention that a dog has attempted to breach the lunch buffet on Deck Fourteen. Needless to say I'll have none of that aboard my ship. There is a brig for both dogs and humans and even though the investment fund that owns this ship has strictly limited my use of these facilities, I am a man of principle and my tolerance is in short supply. The investment fund has also instructed me to say the following regarding weather such as that which we are now experiencing: Though the *Nordic Bliss* has endured similar conditions in the past, past performance is no guarantee of future success. The mariner in me adds the following: The sound that you might be hearing is our triple propeller breaking free of the water each time we crest over these seventy-foot swells. Anyone who is not sick under the conditions has a remarkable constitution and is welcome aboard my crew at any time. For those of you few feeling able, Miss Buttermold, our cruise director, would like you to know that while outdoor activities will understandably be postponed, there will be a full slate of indoor activities starting at oh eight hundred hours and running through the afternoon. Thank you and, remember, keep one hand for the rigging."

The boatswain's whistle blew and Bostitch disappeared, to be replaced by the rain-lashed camera just starting to detect light of dawn in the east.

"We should have flown," Harry moaned and shut off the television.

My Labrador's sleep quota got the better of me, and

I fell into a deep slumber squeezed securely between Harry's bunk and the opposite wall. When I awoke it was still pitch-black because of the lack of a porthole, but I immediately noticed that things seemed calmer.

It occurred to me that my mission for the day must be to address the Tabasco situation. The chief problem was finding a way to communicate with Harry. This time I resolved to search harder for a digital kiosk from which I could send a Virtual Telegram to him. With most people presumably sick in their cabins, this should be possible. Figuring out what to say to coax my owner into action would be another matter.

An hour later Harry and I were at brunch in the Sunshine Salon, which today looked out onto a grim ocean. My owner had placed my two fistfuls of purple food product on a plate under the table next to a large plastic salad bowl full of bottled water.

I chewed slowly in an attempt to make the pleasure of my meager feeding last longer and find what, if any flavor, my new provisions had. But they had none, and then I realized why. The only way to ensure that the pink alarm around my neck would not be triggered was to make food without flavor or smell. Speaking of provisions, I had read a statistic prior to our departure that now came to mind and made me reflect that if my diet did not change soon, I myself would be turning into a four-legged tropical depression. On a cruise of this duration, the *Nordic Bliss* was known to carry twenty-four thousand pounds of beef, twenty-nine thousand eggs, twelve thousand gallons of ice cream, and seventeen thousand slices of pizza. I'm ashamed to admit that my lower natures had begun to claim more and more of the rational and balanced territory in my brain. This silent recitation of food storage facts made me salivate.

Of course, even though a chef stood at the ready behind the omelet bar and another chef at the waffle station, the few passengers in the Sunshine Salon this morning seemed to be eating only unbuttered toast—except for the car salesman from Pasadena, who was working on three omelets at the same time. Blinko's words about Harry's shadow or shadows being ordinary touristic types came back to me now. This man from Pasadena had been popping up quite a bit. I would have to keep an eye on him.

I had only just thought this last part when the car salesman rose, bussed his tray with the wreckage of the three omelets, secured a stack of waffles from the waffle station and had the server drizzle them with lingonberry sauce topped with coddled cream, then walked directly to our table. Harry, visibly wrecked by the weather, was pouring coffee into himself on the vague notion that he had a lecture or a class to teach at some point that morning and this was his preparation. Where Jackson had crafted a manifesto on Rubens and would be armed with a sword-cane against his likely critics, Harry was, per usual, going to use the caffeinated-stream-of-consciousness method to deliver something of value to his listeners.

"Mind if I join you pal?" asked the car salesman from Pasadena, pulling out a chair and sitting down before receiving a reply. His plump legs, stuffed into a pair of tight cream-colored denim shorts with several dozen pockets, many with zippers and bright metal clasps, thrust out into my resting area beneath the table and forced me to relocate, but not before I gathered a generous noseful of Pasadena car salesman. If that was what he was, the car salesman gave off a decidedly crafty scent, one with complex and contradictory layers that suggested both duplicity and cunning. Of course, I reflected as I slumped back down onto my haunches with a huff, most car salesmen would have such a scent. Still, I filed it away in my long mental catalog of aromas for future comparison.

Harry, meanwhile, being too nice as usual, began to speak with this man who had met us at the bon voyage party when my owner had fueled himself with mojitos and I had disgraced myself in the *pigs in a blanket* episode. That was when I had learned his profession and place of residence, but not his name. It was also when he had acquired that sense of possessiveness that people sometimes develop over their shipboard acquaintances. Now that I thought back on it, I remembered noticing the car salesman motion to Harry the day before, just prior to Ivan hollering at my owner to join him. Never a morning person, Harry had missed the salesman, not even acknowledging him.

"Helluva a cruise so far," the man observed. "Thought we were all gonna die last night."

"It was rough," Harry agreed.

"So where you hail from?"

"Manhattan."

"Manhattan." The man whistled as if this were an extraordinary fact. "I've never quite taken to Manhattan."

"People either love it or hate it."

"My mother raised me not to hate anything, but I know I don't love it. Let me put it this way: I dislike it intensely."

"That's too bad."

"No, I don't think so," the man said. "It only means that I'm better suited for where I actually live. I'm a Vermonter, a country boy—Vermont's the Don't Tread on Me state in case you don't know. Brattleboro. I buy and sell farm equipment."

Harry did not seem to pick up the inconsistency in the biography, but his Labrador did. I took another sample of the air around the Californian Vermonter. There was no change in smell. If he was lying it would be impossible to distinguish the individual lies, since lying seemed to be his more or less permanent condition.

"But I told you that already," the man continued.

Harry nodded.

"But you probably don't remember," the man said.

"People don't remember me. That's why I wear these bright shirts."

He gestured at today's Hawaiian top.

"The color's called radioactive orange," he said. "I like the pineapples and the mangos but I could do without the ukuleles."

Harry followed his hand as the man pointed out the various elements that spilled chaotically across his chest.

"I bet you like the ukuleles, am I right?"

"It's a nice shirt," Harry said. He lifted a last fragment of unbuttered toast to his mouth, then thought better of it and put it down.

"Stomach upset?"

"A little."

"I'm eating like a pig. The food is wicked cool."

Harry nodded again and started looking for the exit.

"Geez, here I am talking my head off and I bet you don't even remember my name," he said. "Your name's Harry. You told me that much. But we were both pretty wasted. My name's Frank Booker."

"Good to meet you again, Frank."

"So why you on this ship of fools?" Frank Booker asked as the last of his lingonberry-doused, coddled-cream-topped waffle disappeared into his mouth.

Harry made an obvious show of thinking about his answer. "I just wanted some time away."

"Nice," Booker said. "I won my trip from a radio station and I'm still pinching myself."

"Hoping to get off?"

"Hell no," he said. "The captain's a bit of a nut job, but I'm loving every minute of it. I'm in one of those executive suites. I've got a butler, a Jacuzzi, a panoramic view of the water. I already told you how I'm eating like a pig. Now all I have to do is get me some ladies and they'll never get me off this ship."

"Sounds great."

"So how about you, why you really on this trip? Young guy like you. On your own? With a dog? C'mon, what's the real story?" Booker asked. Harry didn't seem to think much of the persistence, but the persistence was beginning to alarm Harry's dog. I considered some kind of intervention. But Harry sidestepped trouble.

"Just some time away," he repeated. "I thought it would be good to take the hound. They don't do these dog cruises all the time. You don't have a dog, right?"

"Left him at home," Booker said. "But I'm kinda regretting it. Some crazy, cutting-edge stuff happening on board. I mean, I couldn't believe all the dog celebrities they've got. The amount of dog knowledge is so great, you can absorb it just standing around and breathing deep. Heard this one guy—a doctor or scientist or some such—yesterday talk about how dogs navigate through something he called a seventh sense."

"You mean a sixth sense."

"I mean literally a seventh sense. Five senses are for the normal stuff: seeing, hearing, et cetera. Sixth sense

is for the psychic stuff like seeing your dead grand-
mother or visualizing the lottery numbers in a dream.
But according to this guy the seventh sense is psychic-
like but still earthbound enough that it's probably got
something to do with systems we know nothing about
in animals yet . . . biologic systems."

"Like what."

"Like navigation," Booker said. "He told this one
story about a dog that was blindfolded, dropped a hundred miles from its home, and found its way back."

"Maybe it was smell."

"No, there was some reason the guy said why it
couldn't be smell. Stuck a hot iron up the nostrils,
maybe. I forget. Basically, from a purely scientific point
of view there was just no explanation along the lines of
what we understand as possible now."

Booker pointed at me. "I'm telling you, listening to
this guy made me think that there's a lot of stuff hidden
in those brains of theirs and if we just found out what, it
would change the world."

I had heard speculation like this before and never
knew what to make of it. Of course, it was possible, but
Yours Truly had no evidence of great navigational powers on his own part. If anything I had a worse sense of
direction than Harry and frequently found myself completely disoriented in that little domesticated strip of
wilderness in Central Park called the Ramble.

"Interesting," Harry said. "Listen, I think I've got to
go teach a class."

"No problem," Booker said and began to get up as if it were his idea to leave. "Curaçao's the end of the road for you, right?"

Harry was distracted with his tray and answered without thinking.

"I hope so," my owner said before pulling back. "What do you mean the end of the road?"

"Don't some passengers have the option of getting off and flying back stateside instead of doing a round-trip?"

"I didn't know that." Harry had booked without even considering this practicality. He had only imagined the reunion with Imogen and not thought past this to the question of return. Booker's entire air had changed. He had gone from soft, vulnerable, and pathetic into something predatory. It was like watching one of those nature shows in which the rain forest lizard, absolutely still, suddenly snaps out its enormous tongue to catch a cricket.

"So if you only knew about the round-trip, why is Curaçao the end of the road?" Booker insisted.

Harry, who is never good at thinking on his feet, delayed until a serviceable answer appeared. "Sorry," he said. "I guess I wasn't really listening."

Like that lizard after eating the cricket, placidity returned to Booker as if it were his natural state.

"No problem," Booker said. "It's none of my business anyway."

We left Frank Booker and his suspicious interest in Harry's travel plans behind and made our way to that portion of Deck 13 that had been given over to the "slate of indoor activities." There we found Miss Buttermold standing in the middle of the corridor erect and clutching her clipboard.

"Thank God you're here," she said. "Would you believe a little bad weather and everyone falls apart? I've had three lecturers and two workshop leaders cancel. You'd think it was a hurricane. The problem is the captain, he has a way of talking things up and getting everyone scared. It's purely psychological. I believe everything in life is psychological. Actually, I believe that everything is based on the power of want."

"The power of want?"

The cruise director spoke with the zeal of the newly converted. "If you want something in just the right way, with just the right force, and at just the right time, it will happen. It's guaranteed. There's a whole new belief in that now. I'm halfway through the book and I've already wanted *and* gotten an awesome car, a fabulous dress, and an extra week of vacation this year. And it works the other way, too. You don't get what you don't want. I didn't get sick during the storm, for example, or get lost on the subway this time in New York like I did last trip. It works on hiccups, the feminine cycle, and my outbreaks, too. The power of want and the power of don't want. It's going to totally change the world, end poverty, eliminate disease, get rid of dictators, all that good stuff. The author, Jarvis Jejeune, is aboard this ship. He's not much to look at, but the brilliance is just dripping from his pores."

"I've got to get that book," Harry said. Judging by his scent, this was not his intention. His intention and his dog's was to get as far away from Miss Buttermold, her clipboard, and her utopian fantasies as possible. *Utopia* was the Greek word for "no place," and with so much rich abundance of scent and life in the everyday world, a dog knows better than to wish no place was someplace. I would be on the lookout for anyone dripping that kind of brilliance from his pores and go in the opposite direction.

"Dame Norma Aqualung, the famous writer, is on board, too," the cruise director continued. "But to tell you the truth I think she's kind of boring and I don't really understand what she's talking about half the time."

Then Miss Buttermold snapped back to Harry's business. "You're on at eleven hundred hours in Lecture Space Three," she said. "But right now I need you to fill out the audience for Using Your Dog to Find a Mate—Pet Pickup Power in Lecture Space Two. Directly after that, in Lecture Space Five, you're in the audience for Painting Pet Portraits—The Telling Detail."

Harry was about to protest these new additions to his workload, but Miss Buttermold was already off hunting down a passenger who had made the mistake of peeking through a door at the far end of the corridor.

Using Your Dog was being hosted by a man holding a powder-puff canine who kept alternating between licking his face and attending to its nether regions. The man worked at a society magazine in Manhattan and held forth on the usefulness of dogs at our city's dog runs for making "pet-based hookups."

"I had a friend whose Pekingese bit this guy's Great Dane on the ass and that was it. They've been together ever since—the happiest couple I know. I had another friend who…"

The anecdotes paraded out without purpose, evidence of yet another disorganized presentation cobbled together for free passage, and I fell into a light slumber. Harry forced himself to stay awake since he was one of only three people in the audience.

The authority on pet portraits, Ms. Hadley Purcell, was much less painful. This youthful patrician woman of middle years lectured over a canvas set up on an easel in the middle of the room. Her model, a Yorkshire terrier, sat patiently on a cushion in front of the easel, a gingham bow in her hair and a face set to the resigned martyrdom of the professional.

This was Cha Cha.

As I've said, my own face is stone-dead, flapping lips (if you can even call the thin, serrated black flesh that borders my mouth lips), a snout that can express only snarling rage, and soulful but imprisoned eyes. Cha Cha, on the other hand, had features capable of showing everything from disdain to rapture. Her owner told the small, storm-hearty audience that Cha Cha might be a Yorkie, but really she was a *New* Yorkie.

"Cha Cha is what you call an urban sophisticate. When it rains, wears a red raincoat. Doesn't go to the opera, just in case has a fur-trimmed cape. Faux fur because we might be a duchess, but we're a progressive duchess."

Cha Cha's portrait blossomed as she spoke. Dab. Dab. Dab. The gingham bow appeared on the canvas. Dab Dab Dab. Cha Cha's incisive eyes.

"How did Cha Cha get her name?" someone asked.

"Walks down the sidewalk, cha chas."

Dab. Dab. Dab. Cha Cha's ears appeared and then her nose.

"Happy she didn't rumba or Charleston. Lindy or waltz. Polka or jitterbug," she said. "Cha Cha's groomer says he's got a dog that spins called Dervish as in whirling. Great Dane. Stow the china."

She put her brush down. "Now how's our sweetie?" Cha Cha winked.

"So what have I done here?" she asked the audience. "God if I know. You try to capture the spirit. Some dogs easier than others. I'm using watercolors to demonstrate, but oils are my weapon of choice. More depth. More weight. More formal portrait. Master of the hunt.

Lord of the manor. Basset hounds droop off the page in oils. Watercolors everyone's floating away somewhere. But, still, if you want the quick, moment-in-the-life snapshot of the four-legged loved one, watercolors."

Someone cleared his throat at the back of the room. It was Jackson Temple. He was clearly transfixed by the pet portraitist.

"Who is your favorite pet artist of the Northern Renaissance?"

"Rubens," answered Ms. Purcell without pause. "As a well-connected spy, he had access to the exotic animals of Europe's royalty and could study them like no other artist at that time."

"My word." Jackson sighed, heavy with feeling.

Dab. Dab. Dab. A bit of white added the requisite glint of intelligence to Cha Cha's eyes.

After the lecture, Jackson spoke with us in school-boy tones.

"What a magnificent woman," he said. "Even Rubens would be hard-pressed to paint a small dog aboard a heaving ship."

"Why don't you talk with her, Jackson," Harry suggested.

Jackson ground his sword-cane into the carpet.

"It's been such a long time since I've spoken to a woman of such caliber, if ever," he said. "I know I seem like such a public type of person, but I really don't have the faintest idea of how to begin."

"Start with Rubens the animal painter."

"Of course," Jackson said. "And then I can address his collaboration with the famed Flemish animal painter Frans Snyders, noted for his eagles."

"Say that," Harry said and pushed him toward the front of the room and Ms. Hadley Purcell.

I had no time to marvel at Jackson Temple's unexpected infatuation, because there was a commotion in the corridor outside of Lecture Space 5. I walked out into the hallway to see what it was and Harry followed.

Milton Tabasco charged past us muttering obscenities in every direction and shedding the powerful scent of annoyance, an aroma like smoking paper just before it catches fire.

The reason for his annoyance trailed behind him with a cameraman, an audio technician with a boom mike, and another man with a light gun. It was Zest Kilpatrick.

"Mr. Tabasco," she said. "Mr. Tabasco, please stop. We don't want to intrude on your grief, but viewers love you. They want to share your grief with you."

"Leave me alone," Tabasco snarled. "Can't a man keep anything for himself?"

Then Zest revealed a side that I had always suspected was there, but which she had typically kept hidden.

"Look, Tabasco," she said. "You can try to run away but I will track you down. This ship's not that big and no one's getting off for a while. And what a load of garbage. Boo hoo hoo, you need room to grieve. We all know that you were estranged from Kitty and that she was the brains behind your operation and didn't approve of the direction it was going. So you're lucky she had a history of depression and was on meds that made her loopy and made a swim in the ocean at four AM off the back of a ship seem like a good idea. You know you think you're lucky. Do you think I'm the voice of social indignation or justice? I don't care what happened or why she decided to bump herself off. I'm desperate. You're being chased by a desperate woman. I just stood out on deck all night doing satellite uplink for the Storm Channel in a goddamn raincoat ruining a five-hundred-dollar perm when they had to hang me out over the ocean just so I could make the segment more interesting by being hit by a wave. And I prayed—I actually prayed—for the chance to do that because if I don't work I don't even know who I am. Listen, you and I are in a tough business. All that matters is what emotion gets across on that screen, not all the dirty, nasty emotions that get us onto that screen in the first place. I'm desperate because the station's sent me to cover a goddamn pet cruise. Do you think I don't know my career is on the skids? And all because I didn't go to the station director's kid's twelfth birthday party. And I didn't go because I was covering a story..."

Instead of running even farther and faster away from Zest's rant, Tabasco had stopped, turned, and was listening.

"What do you want?" the Dog Mutterer asked.

"I want fifteen minutes with you," Zest said. "I want a sit-down, full emotional recount of what it feels like to lose your beloved partner of fifteen—"

"Twenty."

"Twenty years. I want you to cry. I want you to mutter meaningfully. I want you to show that you hurt."

"I don't."

"Of course you don't," Zest said. "Look, this one interview can get me back in the running, and it won't hurt you, either. Those monks are eating you alive in the ratings. Show why you used to be America's favorite dog trainer and how you're still going forward despite your recent loss and they'll eat it up."

"You don't think it's too soon after her death, do you?" Milton asked.

"No way, it was the day before yesterday."

"Actually it was early morning yesterday."

"Whatever," Zest said. "It's already old news. According to today's infotainment culture, you should already be halfway through the grieving process."

"What else can you offer?" Tabasco asked.

"What else do you want?"

"How about a sit-down interview, full makeup, and walk-around segment showing me working with animals and continuing my and Kitty's mission?"

"Deal," Zest said and then she noticed my owner and blushed. "Oh, Harry."

"Hi, Zest."

"Guess this is just my ambitious side."

"Guess so."

"When can we get this on the air?" Tabasco said.

"In time for the evening news," Zest said. "And if we play this right, I'll bet they'll pick it up nationwide."

"Kitty would be so pleased," Tabasco said.

THE ENCOUNTER WITH MIL-ton Tabasco quickened my resolve to transmit my suspicions to Harry. It might seem as if I had been moving slowly from an investigative point of view and getting too distracted by shipboard life, but in my defense dietary restrictions in an already sluggish Labrador such as myself wreak severe behavioral changes. The two handfuls of purple pellets a day were draining me, as was the near-constant smell of the dozen or so buffets that were steaming all over the ship. I have known of otherwise optimistic animals being thrown into deep ruts of depression from similar deprivation. But the other factor was that there is something about being at sea that seems to stop time and suck the urgency out of things. Kitty's body was floating gently or storm-tossed in the Gulf Stream. Her husband could, as Zest observed, go nowhere for the next few days. A case could be built against him in this time.

Now was the time to contact my owner and get him

involved. The key in the whole matter was not Milton's estrangement from his wife, but his wife's sobbing without ceasing and his scent of bloodthirsty ambition. It was one thing for the infotainment world to know of their estrangement, quite another for me to know of Kitty's sadness and Milton's menacing capacity for violence.

I left Harry to cope as he could with his own lecture on mosaics and hurried off through the still-deserted corridors to find a digital kiosk from which to send my owner an action-provoking telegram. Zest and Tabasco had agreed to wait until the afternoon for their interview and the filming of his work with dogs. The sea was still too rough for any outdoor activities by anyone but intrepid weather reporters, but Captain Bostitch had announced that Tropical Storm Sedadog™ was now zigzagging pinball-like toward the coast of Florida, and we would soon be sailing out from under its waning tail.

I found a digital kiosk on Deck 11 next to one of the darkened gift shops. After a Scandinavian finished polishing the already sparkling glass of the store window and moved on (but not before looking at me as if he could detect each of my hairs as it was shed and each one gave him physical pain), I hopped up onto the seat and attempted to figure out the system.

My experience with Harry's computer keyboard and that dangerous spy-diplomat Leopold Maranovsky had endowed me with some snout coordination and confidence in navigating the electronic environment. I made my way to the video telegram area, clicked on COMPOSE, and soon had hammered out the following in all-lowercase (because I could not use the shift button simultaneous to pressing down the letter keys, and unlike other keyboards this one had no caps lock):

harry, this is spirit guide holmes with an urgent message. milton tabasco involved in the death of his wife. participate with zest in interview and coverage of tabasco and bring dog with you. dog has again been inspired. stay for the entire interview. also beware frank booker. he is too interested in your final destination and might be one of the people shadowing you that blinko warned about. be careful. be suspicious. keep your eyes open, your mouth shut, and your dog close. updates to follow. tell no one of the exact nature of this message.

I reviewed what I had written and thought it sounded like the kind of illiterate Spartan prose that Harry would expect from the spirit world. I wasn't happy to find myself again exploiting his weakness for the occult, and I knew this likely meant Ivan would get involved, but I entered our room number and pressed SEND.

Only after this was done did I realize that a snapshot of Yours Truly had been taken to accompany the video telegram (insurance that would-be pranksters were recorded and could be duly punished). I began to fret, but then concluded that my owner would assume that seeing an image of his dog in connection with this message was nothing other than confirmation of its spiritual origin. I doubted that Harry had any knowledge of the video telegram system or how it worked. The greater challenge would be gaining access to one of these terminals in the future when the ship was bustling again.

The only other problem now was getting Harry back to our cabin so that he could read my message. This would require a direct intervention.

I made my way to Lecture Space 3. Harry was finishing up his presentation. He surprised me with his inventiveness and I admit I felt more than a little ashamed of having underestimated him. Harry had made the small crowd very enthusiastic about the idea of mosaics. In the absence of crafts materials, Harry had made use of the brown paper covering the floor and had illustrated critical aspects of mosaic building by cutting up the paper into shapes held aloft by individuals and then shaping and reshaping patterns by moving the audience around. In between these interactive demonstrations, my owner discussed important aspects of mosaic creation including techniques for kilning mosaic pieces, the kinds of glazing options one had, the ancient origins of the art, and the most successful practitioners. Listening to him, I realize that I often sold my dear Harry short. Perhaps it was just a question

of two males living in such close proximity that com-
petitiveness got the better of one of them—or more
likely how little of this side of himself Harry had shown
in Imogen's absence.

But I didn't have time to reflect on this. The lecture
was ending; he had shaped the audience into a U and
was describing how mosaic tiles were fitted into one another such that the individuals created a pure unity, a
web whose elements support one another honestly
without any material in the seams to cover up mis-
measurement and mistakes. No, I didn't have much
time. He would be finishing up momentarily and then
heading for lunch and who-knew-where-else when he
needed to go back to our room first.

It should be clear that I'm not one for Lassie-style
interventions, but Harry had returned to the podium at
the front of the room where an enormous pitcher of ice
water stood balanced on the ledge. One could almost
feel gravity pulling it earthward.

"So those are the basics of the mosaic craft," my
owner said. "If I conveyed anything, I hope it is
that there aren't any shortcuts to beautiful mosaic work
and…"

His Labrador was charging toward the podium,
tongue awag, ears aflap, and running on an angle with
my head forward.

"You've been a great audience and Randolph…"

But I was already in movement aloft, front paws off
the ground, snout on target. I did a seal-punch of the

pitcher, which slid and then tipped its contents onto my owner.

We walked back to our cabin in silence, the dog's apparent disgrace concealing strategic victory. The video telegram was flashing across the screen when we arrived.

Harry sat down on the edge of the bed and read it as it scrolled.

"What's your photo doing on there?" Harry asked as my face appeared snout-down on the keyboard, eyes looking upward. Fortunately, I had taken the classic canine photograph and looked vacuous and accidental.

Not for a moment did Harry think *mastermind* when he saw that face. Instead, as I had hoped, he immediately reverted to the occult.

"I wonder if Ivan has any of his equipment," he wondered aloud. "The ERPD would be perfect for this."

The ERPD, or the ectoplasmic residual presence detector, looked like an oversized lint brush with red and blue wires leading to a small digital monitor. It supposedly measured the presence of spirits around those they had left behind. Ivan had recently claimed that the device had revolutionized his research. My guess was that the lint brush attachment gathered static electricity and the digital monitor shaped the data to fit improbable ghost-hunting categories on the display such as POTENT SPECTRAL PRESENCE, MODERATE SPECTRAL PRESENCE, MINOR SPECTRAL PRESENCE (tellingly there

wasn't a NO SPECTRAL PRESENCE—in the paranormalist's mind there were always ghosts around). The scientific method might miss a lot in the short run, but at
least it usually limited people's emotions in determining what they discovered. Still, it would be good to have
Harry and Ivan around muddling things on the surface
with their investigations while I did the real work.

Harry snapped on my leash and we left to seek Zest
Kilpatrick and Ivan Manners. We found Ivan first. He
was sitting alone in the corner of Valhalla Vista, the
scene of my humiliation at the hands of Jock Johnson.
Ivan was hunched over a food pile, inhaling chicken on
a stick and thumbing through a catalog. This time when
he saw Harry, he did not shout my owner's name. In
fact, the usually indomitable Manners seemed forlorn.
Even his rainbow lorikeet, Mr. Apples, seemed out of
sorts and stood solemnly by pecking at a small dish of
sunflower seeds that he cracked open very neatly, dis-
carding the husks on Ivan's plate.

"Hello, Ivan," Harry said.

"Greetings," Ivan said. He did not look up from his
catalog.

"How's your cruise?"

"Fine."

"Can I sit down?"

"If you must."

"Something wrong?"

"No."

Harry sat down. Nothing was said for several minutes; the only sounds were the drumming engines, the muffled talk of a handful of diners, and Ivan turning the pages of his catalog. It was exceedingly awkward. Ivan, who usually scented strongly of arrogance—a kind of high-end-cologne smell—now smelled of personal and professional dejection, perhaps even despair. You might have expected this smell to be of the musty-old-shop variety, yet in fact professional dejection when experienced by the very ambitious wasn't the opposite of the smell of arrogance but that smell gone bad. It had a kind of vinegary edge.

"I'm washed up," Ivan said.

"What do you mean?"

"The Dog Mutterer is moving into the paranormal. I've been doing these cruises for a year. My publicist said it would increase my profile to take people on tours, hand out cards, direct them to my television shows and website, build a fan base. It has, but not enough. I've been operating at the mercy of the big players. I thought I had cachet. But I've got nothing like the bloody Dog Mutterer. That guy has his own line of dog biscuits and snow booties."

"What does that have to do with ghosts?"

"He's doing a brand extension," Ivan said. "Apparently, he's saying that his technique is paranormal and qualifies him for doing ghost hunting. It's in the development stage, but I see the writing on the wall. First he'll do something with dead dogs—you know, channeling their spirits for bereaved owners. Next it'll be dog and human ghosts, then it'll just be ghosts. He'll end up owning the bloody territory and I'll have nothing. This guy's an animal. He takes up all the oxygen in the room and then when people are suffocating, he sells it back to them."

"How do you know he's going to do this?"

"I heard him speaking with one of those monks. He was rubbing his hands together. His eyeballs were flashing dollar signs like in the cartoons," Ivan said. "Who was I to dream? I don't even have a master's degree."

Another chicken on a stick disappeared into his mouth like wood being fed into a raging oven.

"Tabasco has his own problems," Harry said.

"You mean his wife?" Ivan said. "He didn't even love her. It was a marriage of convenience. In fact, he's better off without her. I've been talking with Zest."

"You know Zest?" Harry asked.

"Of course. I know all the New York media people," Ivan said. "She was going to do a segment on me but she's decided to do something on Tabasco instead."

"I think I can help you," Harry said.

"I doubt it."

Without revealing the source of his information, Harry said he had learned something important from the other side. Ivan instantly brightened.

"Killed his wife?" Ivan repeated. "That's fabulous. He's going to be dripping with spectral presence."

"Do you have the ERPD?"

"Do I have it? Bloody right I have it. And I have the infrared camera and a dozen other monitors including the ultrasensitive murmur microphone. If that guy has killed his wife, he doesn't have a chance."

Next Harry, Ivan, Mr. Apples, and I set off to convince Zest that we should become a part of her segment. This proved harder than I had expected.

"Harry, you know I'd do anything for you," Zest said. "And I mean anything. But I can't do this. This is an emotion piece. We want to move the viewers. Have them feel for poor Milton Tabasco going on with his life despite the tremendous odds. Suggesting that he pushed his wife over the side doesn't synergize with the narrative of the Dog Mutterer moving forward with his life, brave and alone. This just isn't an investigative piece."

"But you won't have to be investigative," Harry said. "We'll be investigative. All we need to do is hang around while you're with him."

"You, him, the dog, and the parrot," Zest said.

"Rainbow lorikeet," Ivan corrected. "And you were supposed to be filming me anyway."

"Don't push it," Zest said. "So how am I supposed to explain you four?"

"We'll explain ourselves," Ivan said. "Tabasco wants to expand into the paranormal. What better way than joining forces with a well-known ghost hunter..."

"No offense, but you're not that well known, Ivan," Zest observed.

"I might not have my own show, but I *am* a television presence," Ivan said.

"You have something stuck in your teeth," Zest said.

"Chicken," Ivan said.

"And there."

"Pineapple?"

"Got it," Zest confirmed. "What do you two want to do again?"

"We want to stick around for the interview and whatever else you shoot," Harry said. "We'll take some readings."

"You'll be quiet."

"Absolutely."

"If you find anything important, you'll share it with me?" Zest asked.

"Better yet, we'll be a team," Ivan said with renewed confidence.

"Not so fast, cowboy," Zest said. "Not so fast."

TABASCO GOES UNDER THE MICROSCOPE

A DISCERNING DOG DROOLS

ZEST'S WORRIES ABOUT BRING-
ing us along for her interview were unnecessary. At three o'clock that afternoon we
arrived in a large stateroom ablaze with camera lights.
This was Milton Tabasco's suite. Zest and her camera
crew had already gelled the windows against the outside light so that they could get a glimpse of the ocean
roiling behind Milton's head during the piece.

Harry and Ivan were heavily equipped with the
standard ghost-hunting gear about which Yours Truly
had long ago hardened himself against embarrassment.
Still, as we tramped through the ship, I was glad that
most passengers were still sick in their cabins and not
witnessing our paranormal parade (though the Scandinavians preparing an afternoon snack of meatballs and
herring stared as if wondering whether they would have
to clean up after us). Ivan had several tape recorders
hanging from his neck with which to capture spectral
voices, as well as a miner's lamp on his head. He held
the ERPD in one hand and his video camera always set

to infrared in the other. Harry was more understated. He carried a notebook and a backpack stuffed with Ivan's other ghost-hunting miscellany.

Zest had hired the ship's makeup artist, and when we entered Tabasco was having his wrinkles smoothed over with pancake. The harsh and demanding dog-speaking superstar had mellowed into a warm and welcoming uncle. He jumped to his feet and clapped Harry on the shoulder, then looked down at me.

"If it isn't Mr. PLEASE DON'T FEED ME," Tabasco said, reading the letters on the spongy pink monstrosity I had forgotten was still hanging around my neck. Then he addressed Harry.

"Pretty rough weather we've been having, hey, buddy?" Tabasco said. "A lot's gone down since our little dinner together with the captain."

"I'm very sorry about your wife," Harry said.

"I appreciate it," Tabasco said. "But the old girl had a good run and she was a hell of a personality. She couldn't live with herself. You saw how it was at dinner. A little flirty flirty and she lost it. Sometimes the best thing for a person is to stop breathing. The problem with us human beings is we hold on to other people too long. She was ready to move on. She'd been threatening it for years and I always knew she would. Don't get me wrong, I'm going to miss her now and then, but when you operate on my level you go by essentials not senti-mentalities. She's better off and so am I. Not that those people out there in TV land would understand."

Tabasco pointed at the camera lens.

"Those people need love stories and things wrapped up in a pretty bow at the end of the hour. They need stories that make sense because their own stories don't. You and I both know that's just ignorance, but it's how I make my living so there you go. Your friend looks familiar."

"This is Ivan Manners," Harry said. "He's a ghost hunter. He's done some television. They just did a long profile on him in the *Paranormalist*."

"That's where I saw you," Tabasco said, extending his hand. "I am a very big fan of yours."

Ivan blushed. This was something I had never seen except on the rare occasion he drank milk and his lactose intolerance bloomed on his cheeks before he either ran for the bathroom or reached for his inhaler.

"Thank you," Ivan said. "I try to do the best work I can."

"I know you do," Tabasco said. "In fact, I've been thinking of reaching out to you. I'm planning on branching out into the paranormal."

"Really?" Ivan asked as if he hadn't been fuming about this very thing on the walk to the interview.

"My whole Dog Muttering method seems based on that which cannot be explained," Tabasco said. "At first I was a big believer in P.U.S., Positive Unconscious Stimulus. That's where the Tourette's comes in. When I'm talking to our furry friends, I'm basically thinking one thing and saying another. It's trance-like. Fact is, I now believe there's more going on."

"It sounds paranormal," Ivan observed.

"It is paranormal," Tabasco said. "And that's why the next frontier for me is to build on this and reach out to fellow believers. Did you know that sixty-five percent of all adults who own dogs also believe in ghosts, unidentified flying objects, and sorcery? It's the Dog Mutterer's entry to a whole new market of viewers. Bottom line: I'm planning a show that takes me into ghost-hunting, UFO-hunting, witch-hunting situations."

"Makes sense," Ivan said with dark disappointment.

"And I need a team to do it with me. You're my man."

"Me?"

"Who else? As I said, I've been keeping an eye on you. You audience-test high. You're credible. You're brave. You're not good looking enough to challenge the Dog Mutterer with the ladies but not bad looking enough to make them want to change the channel. In short, as this thing develops, I want you as part of the team. And your dog here. He's a must."

Then Tabasco directed a barrage of his trademarked Tourette's syndrome dog-speak at me.

"Corkscrew...lily pad...eponymous...ding-bat..."

As per usual, Yours Truly obeyed whatever message was being sent despite himself. More commands followed, and soon I found myself on my back pawing the air like a show pony. Here I was in the presence of a man I distrusted, a man who had threatened me just a day earlier, and I was exposing my soft belly against my will.

"He's not my dog," Ivan said. "But if you've got to have him, I'm sure Harry'll be all for it."

"I don't think Randolph's ready for the big time just yet," Harry said. "At heart he's a homebody."

I looked up at Harry, who responded by locating a clock on the wall, digging in his back pocket, and emerging with my day's second fistful of purple food product.

"Dinner," he said, kneeling down in front of me with his palm open. I ate gratefully, and he gave me a pat on the head.

Ivan was happy. Tabasco seemed relaxed, though this was relative because the strength of his ambition hung over everything even now. The ghost hunters set up their equipment after briefing Tabasco on their intention to catch traces of his late wife during the interview. The makeup artist finished pancaking Tabasco's deep wrinkles and then lifted lint and stray hairs off his shoulders with duct tape. Zest sat opposite him and fingered through her notes. Mr. Apples began to make a racket. Ivan—despite his outspoken advocacy for the bird—locked him in the bathroom. Yours Truly sat down on his haunches out of the frame but in smelling range.

Zest began with the usual infotainment softballs. She asked about how Tabasco met his wife, what he first

thought when he saw her, if there were any funny stories. He was powerfully entertaining and hit just the
right balance between dewy-eyed reflection and sudden bursts of seemingly unscripted humor. Reality is
quirky; the best con artists know this and add all the
right surprises and flaws to make their versions believ-
able.

Harry and Ivan bustled about taking readings
around Tabasco and flashing each other significant
looks that presumably indicated spirits were in the
room. I sifted through the scents Tabasco shed. He
worked through his bio: building their Dog Muttering
venture, the early years when the money was tight, the
middle years when fame had its consequences on their
relationship, and the later years when basking in a ma-
ture romance there were walks on the beach and quiet
intimacies.

For this last part—a raging lie, as everyone in the
room knew—Tabasco reeked of the usual aroma of de-
ceit. Then Zest asked the Dog Mutterer to relive the
night of Kitty's death. I prepared myself to parse
through the scents that I knew were central to the
question of what had happened that night. Zest was
merely seeking an innocent reenactment; I was listening and sniffing for a reenactment that I was certain
would disprove his innocence.

"And so Kitty left the dining room that night and
went for a walk?" Zest asked.

"I saw her leave the dining room. Where she went I

have no idea," Tabasco said. Suddenly the Dog Mutterer was uncharacteristically hesitant. "You're not going to use this, are you? You and he both saw how she left, and I didn't see her after that. But I don't know if it's all that wonderful to tell our fans that the last time we saw each other she was giving me hell, then stalked off somewhere and I didn't follow her."

"Don't worry about it," Zest said. "We'll edit the story around the image we want to project, not the facts. I'm a professional, Milton. You're gonna look great."

I inched forward barely aware of this exchange and much more aware of Tabasco's statement that he had not seen Kitty again that night. This was—my nose did not deceive—undeniably true and a staggering surprise.

"And just to repeat, that was the last time you saw Kitty?" Zest asked.

"Yes."

The soundman who was also the field producer motioned for Zest to ask Tabasco to restate.

"Could you repeat that as a complete sentence?" Zest asked.

"Sure. And that was the last time I saw Kitty."

Again, the scent was one of unassailable truthfulness. If Milton Tabasco had not seen Kitty again that evening, how could he have pushed her over the side?

"When did you first realize something was wrong?" Zest asked.

"Oh, it must have been four AM," Tabasco said. "I was right here in this stateroom, asleep, and I suddenly woke up because the ship had stopped. Through that window right behind me I could see a spotlight dancing across the water, and there was some shouting. Then a little after that I heard a helicopter and the ship started up again. Somehow I knew she was gone, but I couldn't admit it to myself."

Tabasco shed contradictory scents. There was truth. There was lie. The conflicting odors inundated my nose and brain and I struggled to separate them. I was almost certain he had not been in his stateroom as he maintained, not experienced the events as he recited (there was a sort of blank smell that suggested not a lie but a later reconstruction of the memory), but in terms of his feeling that something had been wrong...that seemed like the truth. And all through this thicket of contradictory aromas was suffused the bloodthirsty ambition that I had detected around Tabasco since the beginning.

"How did you know that everything wasn't okay?" Zest asked. "Because she wasn't here?"

"No, it wasn't that," Tabasco said. "Kitty's always been a free spirit. It's natural that if she's on this ship, she wouldn't come home until dawn. She'd be out doing new things, experiencing something different. That was my Kitty."

"So what was it?"

"What can I say?" Tabasco said and began to apply

the misty-eye treatment again. "You live with someone long enough and you're attached to them on a whole different level. That was the way it was between Kitty and me."

"So what happened then? You got up right away?"

"I did not get up right away," Tabasco said. "I lay there and tried to get back to sleep, but my sense that something was wrong just grew and grew until finally I just had to get up. So I did. I put some clothes on. I went out onto the deck. Something brought me to the back of the ship. It must have been five or five thirty because I remember that the sun was already coming up. Anyway, there were a lot of the crew gathered there with the captain, and he was telling them how it was unacceptable that anybody could be lost overboard. So I went up to him and asked him who went overboard and…"

Tabasco paused, and the eyes that had been dewy throughout this telling now began to fill with tears. He bent forward, then held his hand up to the camera as if to block its intrusion into his grief.

"I'm sorry," he said.

None of this was real. All of Tabasco's sorrow from the start of his story was as synthetic as the pancake makeup starting to glisten with sweat under the lights. He asked for a drink of water.

"I guess even if you think you're estranged, the emotion is all right there," Tabasco said, fixing Zest with a

hard stare. Zest, who was also tearing up, nodded and
dabbed at her eyes with the sleeve of her blouse.
Tabasco continued.

"So, as I said, I approached the captain and asked
him that question and he described my wife. There had
been a witness, someone who had actually seen her do
it, I forget her name, a singer or something, Vicki
LaBloom…"

My Labrador ears perked up. *Vicki LaBoom, not
Vicki LaBloom,* I thought. *Vicki LaBoom, legendary star
of Broadway stage and cabarets worldwide. Singer of
blues, jazz, and classic favorites such as "Sunny Side of the
Street"… Mover of canines to sublime musical heights never
before reached…* Vicki LaBoom had witnessed Kitty's
demise. I had been waiting for mention of the tardy
witness, the irresponsible observer who had waited too
long to stop the ship. In my mind I had already con-
nected this dubious person to the death and had
posited in them either a faulty memory, an incomplete
vantage point that missed some crucial detail (such as
Milton Tabasco lurking in the wings or delivering the
fatal shove), or, most sinister, some role in causing the
death. But not Vicki LaBoom. Vicki LaBoom was personally unpalatable as the witness and also, I reflected,
objectively unbelievable.

"LaBloom described Kitty to a T. Only one person
could have worn that hairdo, and no one on the planet
had that blue reflective jacket she had custom made in

Milan where we went to renew our marriage vows. Now it's gone with Kitty."

"So you knew then," Zest asked.

"I knew then," Tabasco said.

"And what did you do?"

"I told the captain that I believed that it was my wife who had gone overboard. He accepted it."

"He accepted it just like that?" Zest asked, her reporter instincts, dormant since she had stepped aboard the *Nordic Bliss,* getting the better of her. "I mean, shouldn't they do a roll call or something?"

"I don't know," Milton Tabasco said. "My guess is that there is some rule about it. Anyway, disembarking at the next port is pretty airtight. No one even steps off the boat until all the passengers are accounted for."

"How do you know that?" Zest asked.

Tabasco hesitated again. "Doesn't everybody?"

"Let's get back to that moment," Zest said.

"Sure, why not," Tabasco said and shifted in his chair, reeking of exactly the kind of sinister untrustworthiness that you'd expect to find in a suspect during one of those cinematic crime drama interrogations.

Zest overlooked the body language in favor of the human interest angle—love, loss, and hope.

"I want to really feel what that early-morning exchange was like for you. After all, here you are a man married for twenty years to this woman."

"Twenty-eight, actually," Tabasco said.

"A long time," Zest gushed.

"A long time."

"And there she is, your wife of so many years, somewhere out there, floating in the vast dark ocean with the ship propellers chopping at whatever might have fallen into them and the sharks hunting and the killer whales killing and the jellyfish doing whatever it is that they do... I can't even comprehend it. Could you reconstruct that moment for us?"

As absurd as Zest's feature reporter's zeal to squeeze emotion out of the Dog Mutterer was, the cross-examination was providing Yours Truly with a great deal of smell information. Tabasco, the unflappable, was now Tabasco the nervous and uncertain. His wiggling around in his seat was matched by olfactory crosscurrents. I smelled a great deal of internal waffling going on. The smell of waffling is surprisingly like the smell of waffles—so similar, in fact, tha⁺ I began to think about waffles. Once I had them with butter and maple syrup—Harry had ordered the farmer's breakfast from our local diner and then slipped me some of the leftovers. I had not had a waffle since, and had hoped to enjoy one aboard ship at the breakfast buffet, but Jock Johnson and his dietary tyranny had ruined those plans.

"Your dog is drooling on my shoe," Tabasco observed, shocking me back to this world. "I wouldn't mind but they're three-thousand-dollar Italian loafers."

He wiped his three-thousand-dollar Italian loafers with a handkerchief.

"Randolph," Harry said. "Go there."

He pointed at the far corner of the room. I hesitated against the powerful tug of obedience. How could I have let my stomach run away with me again? Needless to say, I was very disappointed in myself. The origin of the word *waffle,* as in to be undecided, to waver, to flip-flop, isn't even related to the delicious breakfast food. It is from the Anglo-Saxon *waff,* to blather.

"Randolph," Harry repeated. "Go to that corner."

"Oh, it's okay," Tabasco said. "Let him stay there. He's a great audience. You really get a sense that he's listening. Either that or he thinks I'm dinner. I'll just keep my shoes out of the way."

Then he turned to Zest. "We still rolling?"

The cameraman nodded.

"Good," Tabasco said. "Let me tell you exactly how I felt . . ."

The Dog Mutterer spoke of the moment on deck after Kitty's disappearance with such poetry and drama that for a moment even I found myself wanting to believe that what I heard was true even though I knew it was a lie — such is the power of the word. Tabasco told Zest of screaming Kitty's name, being restrained by sturdy Scandinavian sailors as he tried to hurl himself into the sea, Captain Bostitch's prudent actions and strong example of leadership, and finally of his own epiphany that if it was time for Kitty to move on, he must let her. All of this, from discovery of his lost mate to cathartic resolution, clocking in at less than three hours "real" time, two minutes twenty-four seconds "screen" time.

It would make dramatic television.

"Oh, my." Zest sighed, perhaps moved by the ratings potential. "What a story."

But she was not allowed to linger in this warm place. Ivan Manners was agitated.

"We've got major ectoplasmic activity around his left ear," Ivan barked and then began videotaping in infrared.

"Please don't step on my lines," Zest said. "Silence after saying something thoughtful always works on-screen."

Ivan ignored her.

"This is something," Harry said. "Historic readings."

Even Tabasco seemed interested.

"Is she here?" he asked.

Ivan did not answer. Instead he removed a polished instrument from a black case. It looked like something that gets stuck in the Thanksgiving turkey, with a nail-like protrusion capped by a dial. In fact it *was* an oven thermometer, jerry-rigged by Manners to detect minor changes in temperature due to supernatural activity.

"Can I place the probe inside your ear?"

"Why not?"

Ivan whistled significantly.

"Something," he said. "Definitely something. Proceed."

Ivan removed the probe, and the interview resumed.

"So what are you going to do now?" Zest asked.

"I'm going to further Kitty's memory," Tabasco said. "But tonight, my dear, I am going to perform magic and all of you are invited to come."

THE DOG MUTTERER PERFORMS

———————

ENTER THE IMPOSSIBLE MURDER

I WILL BE THE FIRST TO admit that I'm a middling to poor detective, and if this is a detective tale I am supposed to have been recounting then it is really not a first-rate one at all. If you have paid good money for such a story, demand your money back at once. The sad fact is that I am hobbled by my canine limits just as much as I am aided by some of its advantages.

Excuses could be made for my flight of fancy at the mention of waffles or my irrepressible, loafer-ruining drool. I could say that Jock Johnson was to blame. But like most sentient beings, I suppose I like to think myself better than I actually am. Maybe it is a safer and more comforting way of living. Maybe I have no choice. Maybe there is always a dark night of the soul waiting to turn me into a trembling, anxious mess. It would be easier to have that solid identity to don than all of this uncertainty about who it is exactly I am.

Still, if I am a detective, it is in the tradition of some of those literary detectives. Holmes, Marple, Poirot (the name means "fool" in French) were essentially all amateurs and all beset with several failings each—Poirot is especially beloved by me for his pomposity and his love of bonbons. But the one thing these fictional types had that I do not were well-crafted mysteries within which they could perform lovely acts of smooth, efficient detection. Marple could notice that a watch was being worn on the wrong wrist and make the clever deduction that, like a key in the door, would unlock the puzzle. Holmes could read the newspapers like a code that only needed decryption.

But I don't have these crafted playgrounds; all I have is my undependable and sometimes embarrassing self and the messy reality that you and I both share. Sometimes, however, things actually function like a work of detective fiction.

Such were the events that followed Milton Tabasco's declaration about doing magic.

At eight o'clock that night, Harry and I were once again in the theater. This time the space was filled with passengers. Tropical Storm Sedadog™ had moved off to the east to ravage another stretch of ocean. The sky at sunset was ruby red.

"Red sky at night, sailor's delight," Captain Bostitch had proclaimed over the ship's communications system, apparently reconciled to the prospect of good weather. Of course, he was able to first delight in recounting the damage done to the ship's interior by the heaving storm waves and the still-overflowing infirmary, which no seasickness medication could address.

We were gathered in the theater to see Milton Tabasco, the magician. Well before his career training dogs, he had been an amateur illusionist, and for a lark and to escape from the heaviness of recent events he wanted to return if only for one night.

"You see, that's how I got my start," Tabasco had told Zest as her cameraman packed up his equipment and Harry and Ivan conferred about matters paranormal.

"But there was no money in it and I wasn't all that good. Good enough to do some of the small venues in Vegas, but not good enough to be a regular, have my own show, and you need your own show to make it work. But now with my celebrity, my agent thinks that I can expand back into magic. So I'm trying it out here. To be one hundred percent honest, I'm pretty nervous. You should definitely have your cameras there. You never know what can happen."

Zest's cameras were there. She was sitting next to Harry in the front row, but had decided that at most the performance would be b-roll for what she was now calling her Tabasco profile. After the sit-down interview, we had followed the Dog Mutterer through a late-afternoon class in which he turned a dozen Jack Russells with behavior problems into model citizens. Footage of that class would fill out Tabasco's remarkable growth for the television audience. Zest seemed well pleased with how her cruise was shaping up.

"I know it's horrible to say, but when it comes to making a story work, there's nothing like death. Poor Kitty," Zest said, reaching out to brush her fingertips along Harry's thigh but instead touching only a loyal Labrador's coat.

Before Harry could answer, the lights had dimmed and the curtain rose. A deep male voice announced:

"Ladies and gentlemen, please welcome the star of television's *The Dog Mutterer*, the Dog Mutterer himself, Milton Tabasco, performing in an exclusive, one-night-only, world-premiere engagement. You know him as a magician with dogs, but tonight you will meet Tabasco the mind-bending, reality-defying illusionist. Milton Tabasco."

Milton Tabasco, dressed in a tuxedo with a bright red cape, ran onto the stage. The audience roared. A few dogs barked and continued to bark long after the cheers and applause had died.

"Pequot . . . fireside . . . manhandler," Tabasco said, and the dogs fell silent.

He began with some jokes delivered stand-up-comic-wise from the proscenium and, still joking, waded into his first tricks—standard magic, playing-card fare. Things got more complicated when he invited a husband and wife from the audience to participate. After sealing Janice, the wife, in a soundproof booth, he proceeded to have David, the husband, mark

several cards, which to everyone's surprise Janice somehow possessed when she exited the booth. Tabasco
kept up the social and comedic patter, delighting audience and volunteers except for Captain Bostitch, who
was forced onto the stage by his wife and then had his
pocket watch—inherited from a nineteenth-century
whaling master Bostitch—disappear only to reappear
out of his ear after he had flown into a fury.

"Let's hear it for our captain and his temper.
Smooth sailing," Tabasco said as Bostitch stormed off
the stage, ranting that he belonged back on the bridge.

This brought us to the finale. Two cages with steel
bars flashing in the stage lights were wheeled onto the
stage by a pair of men dressed in black. Tabasco circled
the cages, yanked at the bars, tested their strength.

"I need a man and his dog," Tabasco announced.
"And a word of warning: Whoever comes up here must
be ready to cease to be for a split second, to travel
through time and space. Because whoever comes up
here will find themselves in one of these cages one moment and in the other cage the next. Let's see some
hands."

Zest grabbed Harry's hand and raised it high.

"Come on, folks. Someone's got to be curious about
the fourth dimension," Tabasco said.

"Him, him, him," Zest cried. Harry did not want the
attention and tried to lower his arm, but Zest was determined. Her raspberry-colored nails dug into my
owner's hand.

"Come on," she said. "It'll be fun."

Tabasco's eyes fell upon us as if we had always been his intended targets. "You two," he shouted. "Up here on the double."

Harry cringed in his seat, but Tabasco led the crowd in a chant. Reluctantly, we went. The size of the crowd and the vast expanse of space made my tail burrow itself between my legs.

Naturally Tabasco acted as if he had never seen us before and used my plumpness to again play to the crowd.

"I only needed one dog," he said. "Seriously, you've got to stop feeding this guy."

Then he "noticed" the pink sign hanging down from my neck and to predictable roars and multiple guffaws, he read its words aloud. To make things worse, my tail, as per usual out of my control, began wagging wildly because Tabasco had scratched me under the ear as he read.

Tabasco then stood up, dramatically fluttered his black-and-crimson cape, and at a jog traced a figure eight around the two cages.

"Do you know what I'm going to do?" he asked Harry.

"No," Harry said. My strapping owner who usually stood so straight and tall was hunched forward and had dug his hands deep into the pockets of his jeans.

"You don't say a lot, do you?" Tabasco said.

"Not really," Harry said. "I'd like to disappear."

"Well, that's exactly what you and your faithful hound are going to do," Tabasco said and motioned Harry to the closer cage. "You're a strong-enough-looking lad. Go ahead and climb right in."

Harry did as he was told. The opening was comically small, and he bumped his head loudly on the bars.

"Watch yourself," Tabasco said. He made a show of locking my owner in with a giant padlock and enormous skeleton key. Then a Scandinavian girl attired in a crimson one-piece swimsuit appeared onstage and presented Tabasco with a pole. He took the pole, delivered a gawking conspiratorial once-over to his assistant and a rakish wink to the crowd, and then raced around the cage dramatically poking above, below, and along the sides to show that it was free of "hidden compartments or any other illusionist's mechanism." While he did this, his assistant began to spin the cage, which was on wheels.

"Hold on, my friend," Tabasco said.

Harry gripped the bars as the assistant spun the cage faster and then began to move it around the stage.

"And now for you," Tabasco said, picking up my leash and leading me up to the second cage. Standing before the opening, he looked at me and hammed bafflement to the crowd. He dipped down as if to pick me up, but thought better of it. He scratched his head. He looked off into the wings as if thinking. Meanwhile in the other cage, Harry—who had just gotten past seasickness from the storm—looked as if he was slipping.

The swimsuited assistant reappeared with a rolling set of stairs.

"Perfect," Tabasco exclaimed and led me up into the cage. "Atta boy."

This went against my sensibilities, but I couldn't let Harry go alone. I, too, was locked in, my cage poked, prodded, and spun around. A few moments later two satin sheets descended from wires above us and completely covered both our cages. My cage was spun again. I struggled to stay on my feet and from a distance heard a drumroll. This was most unpleasant and on top of the sheer sensations, my overweening sense of responsibility made me feel somehow accountable for the success of the trick. After all, I thought, I had read about magic before and seen a handful of magicians perform on television, including one who made the Statue of Liberty "disappear," but typically these things seemed to require some kind of participation. Didn't most magicians "disappear" their assistants? And even if Harry was instructed to go along with the trick, no one could expect the same from me. The drums continued to roll, the cage continued to spin. I sat down on my haunches. So dizzy, I lay down on the floor of the cage. But still the cage spun. I wondered if Harry was being given the same treatment. And then a strange thing happened. I heard a distinct metallic click, the ship's orchestra blared something triumphant, and with a sound like a coiled spring being released, the floor dropped out from beneath me and I found myself falling onto the stage and into a spotlight.

As Yours Truly tried to steady himself before crumbling into a heap, the crowd applauded. I was aware of Tabasco and his assistant whisking the covers off the cages above my head and then the Dog Mutterer shouting.

"Ladies and gentlemen," he said. "A surprise visitor: my wife, Kitty Tabasco."

I had heard wrong. The trick and too little food had diminished my senses. Then I heard a gasp, one of those great, collective inhalations that you think happen only in books. But it was real, and my olfactories were filled with the smell of the crowd. It had shifted from amusement and distraction to disbelief slipping into horror.

I staggered to my feet and craned to see what everyone else was staring at. Milton Tabasco had frozen. A look of triumph was pasted to his face but his eyes seemingly registered shock (though I did not smell the shock). He and everyone else in the theater, including a still-imprisoned Harry, the orchestra band members, and the spotlight operators high up in the ceiling, were all gaping at Kitty.

I had heard right. Tabasco had indeed pronounced his wife's name.

Kitty Tabasco, extravagantly coiffed and wearing an outfit that matched her husband's, lay dead with a dagger sticking out of her back on the floor of the cage I had just occupied.

"Kitty," Milton Tabasco shouted and began to cry. "Kitty, baby. Wake up. Kitty, baby."

Someone in the audience screamed. Tabasco's Scandinavian assistant fainted in a dead drop right onto the stage. Then just as it seemed that everything would somehow be frozen forever, everything started to move very quickly. Tabasco jammed the oversized skeleton key into the giant padlock and wrenched open the door. He leaped inside and cradled his wife, whose back was drenched with blood from the knife wound. The orchestra began to play again and the curtain dropped, sealing us off from the audience.

It was a strange feeling to go from the exposed stage to the intimacy of this narrow enclosure. The lights went up and people began to fill the space in the way that people do after a catastrophe, lending a sense of assistance even though there was nothing for most of them to do but watch and mumble to one another. At some point someone heard Harry rattling on his cage door and released him. By now, Zest Kilpatrick and her camera crew were on the scene shooting, Ivan Manners was recording paranormal disturbances, someone calling himself a hotel detective had arrived, and Captain Bostitch was said to be on his way back down from the bridge.

Meanwhile Tabasco held his dead wife and sobbed without ceasing. I could not get close enough to assess the sincerity of his grief, but I was close enough to smell that Kitty was only freshly dead. The woman had clearly not been lost at sea. I took a deep snout sample of the underside of the cage on which, as I now recognized, her scent was impressed.

"This will not do," Captain Bostitch boomed as he approached Tabasco in the cage. "I will not have people jumping off my ship and then coming back to life only to get jiggered in the back during an entertainment. Utterly without precedent, this."

"Captain Bostitch," said the man who had identified himself as the hotel detective. He had already given out a dozen or so of his musical business cards, which when opened played the theme song from a familiar crime drama.

"Who the bloody hell are you, sir?"

"I am the answer to your prayers."

"I doubt it."

"Are you getting all of this?" Zest directed, pulling her audio tech until his furry boom mike was hovering mere inches above Captain Bostitch's head.

"Oh, but Captain, I know of the recent cutbacks your line has had and the unfortunate timing—"

"Stop blathering and get to the point."

"I'm a hotel detective from Las Vegas. You've just let your ship's detective go. There is a corpse with a dagger in her back. My name is Raphael Santorini. Let there be commerce between us."

Santorini pushed a musical card into Captain Bostitch's hand, and it began to play.

"Good Lord," Captain Bostitch said. He looked the hotel detective up and down. "Las Vegas, you say?"

"I've seen it all."

"This you haven't seen," Captain Bostitch said. "Very well. Come along."

Soon there was a small crowd gathered around the cage along with Milton Tabasco, who was still sobbing. From time to time he would lift Kitty's limp arm only to let it drop back down.

"I want this stage clear of all inessential personnel," Captain Bostitch roared. Within seconds the crowd had thinned to Zest, her crew, three stagehands, Harry, Ivan, the Scandinavian assistant in the bathing suit—by now revived—whose name was Inge, Milton Tabasco, Santorini, and Yours Truly, positioned between the captain and the hotel detective.

At first no one, not even the captain, knew what to say. Then Santorini cleared his throat and circled the cage once in as dramatic a fashion as Tabasco had done himself only fifteen minutes earlier. He stopped, cleared his throat again, and addressed the assembled.

"What we have here is that rarity of rarities in the annals of homicide: the so-called impossible crime."

KITTY TABASCO HAD BEEN laid on a gurney and covered with Milton Tabasco's crimson cape so that only her impossibly long stiletto heels protruded from the bottom and at the top the crown of her impossibly structured hairdo. The ship's doctor had pronounced her dead while Tabasco had still been with her in the cage. Our small group of witnesses had been asked to sit in the front rows of the now empty theater.

Santorini cut a curious figure. He was short and wore a peach-colored suit with wide lapels and a carnation in the buttonhole; his cheeks twitched and eyes blinked as if he were staring into a bright light that followed him wherever he went. Frankly, it would have been hard to take him seriously if he didn't speak with such clarity and conviction. But he did, and from those first moments it became clear that Raphael Santorini would be the one designated to explain what had just happened.

"The 'impossible crime' is exactly what it sounds

like," he began, ignoring Milton Tabasco, who stared with blank eyes into the middle distance. "I will need to speak with all of you at some point, but let me begin with defining what I have just said. Some of you will be familiar with the term *impossible crime* from detective fiction. In this genre, the impossible crime is also known as the 'locked room' mystery. That is, a crime is committed in a locked room or a place—such as this cage—with no visible means of entrance or exit for the murderer. On the surface, the fact of Kitty Tabasco's murder seems impossible."

"Kitty, baby," Milton Tabasco wailed.

"I speak for everyone, I know," Santorini continued addressing the Dog Mutterer, "when I say how deeply sorry I am for your loss tonight."

Tabasco's eyes flickered acknowledgment like a Morse code light signaling from far away.

"Yes, there is no one aboard this ship who is not shocked and saddened by your loss," Santorini said. "Let me revise—you will excuse my lack of delicacy: Saddened most of your fellow passengers are ... Shocked at the death none of us are. For we have been sad about this death for two days and are only shocked by the fact that your wife appears to have died twice. This adds considerably to the concept of an 'impossible crime.' "

As Santorini spoke, I thought back on the snout sample I had recently gathered from Kitty. There was nothing waterlogged about it. Additionally, there were two elements that I could not reconcile: an almost giddy excitement, coupled with the rapid onset of what I could only describe to myself as a "knowing horror"— a horror that was primal and cataclysmic and made worse by a revelation of some kind. The last moments of Kitty's life, I concluded, had been complicated.

Santorini circled back to fill in more details of the "impossible" crime.

"To the average observer," he said, pausing dramatically in stock detective fashion (I almost expected him to hold up a finger), "it actually seems impossible that a murder could have been committed at all. For example, there is the body with a gunshot wound but no gun and the doors and windows locked from the inside. The windows without evidence of a bullet passing through them. Or, in our case, a corpse in a cage with a dagger in its back and a thousand sets of eyes trained on that cage at the moment of the murder seeing nothing and no means behind the crime."

"Oh, Kitty, poor baby," Tabasco moaned.

Santorini continued. "To the casual observer, who is commonly quite superstitious, it appears that supernatural forces may be at work. It is up to the consummately rational mind of the detective to prove that the impossible crime is indeed deducible. In the present case, I find inspiration in the great detective writer John Dickson Carr, who in his classic *The Problem of the Wire Cage* used a fenced-in tennis court to illustrate the problem."

"My poor wife lying there dead and murdered," Tabasco cried. "And all you can do is talk about tennis?"

"Mr. Tabasco, I understand your pain, but there are clear parallels here, and for us to conduct a proper investigation we must determine exactly how impossible your wife's death appears on the surface. Literary precedents are critical."

"For God's sake, do get on with it," Captain Bostitch said. "We all understand how bloody unlikely it is, and in all my years at sea I've never had a passenger bumped off other than that shuffleboard love triangle murder. Unfortunate, that, but at least they did things with style back then. He, I believe, was a Lord, though neither of his birds were ladies, I'm afraid."

"I implore your patience, but method must be methodical," Santorini said.

I am ashamed to say it, but I had begun again to drift into thoughts of food and was just then imagining the tang of the sparerib sauce employed by our local Chinese restaurant. It was the sesame oil, I concluded, that made the ribs so irresistible. That and a touch of vinegar. My empty stomach trembled with the memory of such delight. I moved my head away from Harry's leg in case I began to drool again.

"This is a most painful request," Santorini said. "But in the name of method, I must ask the first question of you, Mr. Tabasco."

"What the hell is it?"

"You are a magician. These devices—the two

cages you were preparing to use in this trick—do in fact contain compartments in which to secrete or hide individuals—or dogs—who will appear to disappear and reappear. Is this correct?"

Tabasco nodded.

"At this point I trust that it is all right to ask you how this device works."

"Magicians never reveal their tricks," Tabasco said.

"Come now, Mr. Tabasco, your wife has been murdered. Besides, these cages are widely available on the magician's market. I have actually inspected a cage similar to yours in Vegas."

"Similar, not the same."

"Perhaps," Santorini said, a harder tone coming into his voice. "But that is not the point. Your wife is dead, and that cage is involved somehow."

"You're right," Tabasco said. "I'll tell you. The cage is designed with a floor that revolves. It has a special compartment that holds the person who will appear and conceals the person who will disappear. For this particular act, I modified the device so that the dog dropped directly onto the floor instead of being revolved into the hidden compartment."

This explained the metallic click, the sound of the spring, and my tumble to the ground.

"So you never had any intention of having the dog and his owner switch places in the cages?"

"No. That was a cover for the real trick," Tabasco

said, his typical impatience creeping in. "Let me explain since you're obviously going to go there anyway. I
knew Kitty was in the cage. I announced it, didn't I?
Moreover, these guys knew Kitty was in the compartment."

Tabasco pointed at the three stagehands. "Isn't that
right, boys?"

The three men nodded. One of them said, "We
helped put her inside just before the cages were moved
onstage."

"And she was alive and well then?"

"If you mean that she didn't have a dagger sticking
out of her back, yes," the same man answered.

"This leads me to another point," Santorini said.

Tabasco interrupted. "Why did I let the whole ship
believe that Kitty was dead if I knew that she was
alive?"

"Exactly."

"Here, here," Captain Bostitch said. "If the lass was
never overboard, it's not cricket to pretend that she
was. Do you know that each time the Coast Guard as-
sists in a rescue, they send us the bill? Fifty thousand
colonial dollars. Well, sir, be warned that I will be for-
warding that tidy debt to you."

"I won't pay it," Tabasco said.

"And why not?"

"Because I was conned as much as the rest of you."

"But you knew that she was alive," Santorini said.

"Yes, two hours before the show, but not before that."

"Even if you knew one hour before the show, why didn't you alert the authorities?"

Tabasco began to cry again. Zest gestured to her cameraman, who had been continuously filming, to zoom in for a closeup.

"Do you know what it's like to worry that you're losing your audience and that you're never going to get them back? I fought for every one of those people out there watching me tell them about dogs and, frankly, we've been getting killed in the ratings. We just don't have that edge anymore. I thought this would give us some badly needed hype. It's all about hype—forget trying to actually give people something of real value. Our culture's not about that anymore. The monks are absolutely slaughtering us and you know that adage about bad publicity being better than no publicity. Absolutely true. Did you know that the monks have gotten their orange schnapps banned on one hundred and fifty-four college campuses? I mean, you can't have better publicity than that. For every ban, schnapps sales increase and they go up in the ratings."

Santorini looked confused.

"And so how does this apply to the current situation?"

"It doesn't get much clearer," Tabasco said. "Kitty jumping out and screaming *I'm alive* in a magic trick after everyone thinking she's dead—now, that's bad publicity. I look bad. She looks bad. People talk about it for days. Our ratings go way up. Magazines do profiles on us as troubled or making us look shameless. One of us might even get arrested. But at least they're talking when, in this world, all the gravity is pulling us back to silence."

"Yes, I've got it," Santorini said. "But why did you know only two hours before the show?"

"You'd have to ask her," Tabasco said. "This is what I think happened. First night on board and we were having an argument over the usual."

"The usual?"

"I like the ladies and Kitty didn't like that I liked the ladies. Most of the time she'd be angry for ten minutes then we'd move on. But not this time. This time she decided that she had the opportunity to teach me a lesson. She decided to make it seem like she had jumped overboard, then she hid for a few days."

"She must have been very angry."

"Every relationship is a world unto itself," Tabasco said and began to cry again. "Oh, Kitty, baby."

"So permit me to rehash what we know," Santorini said. "Kitty Tabasco never jumped overboard."

"Bloody cheek, that," Captain Bostitch muttered.

"She was alive when she got into the hidden compartment in the cage and she was put into the compartment by . . ."

"No one," one of the stagehands said. "I watched her climb in by herself."

"And Mr. Tabasco did not help?"

"He wasn't anywhere around," the stagehand said. "A few minutes later we pushed the cages out onstage."

"Did you check on Ms. Tabasco between the time that she climbed into the secret compartment and the time you pushed the cages out onstage?"

"No," the stagehand said. "But she was talking. I don't think she ever stopped talking—until now. She was cracking jokes. Dirty jokes."

"That's my Kitty," Tabasco said.

Santorini again addressed the group.

"So we know that Kitty Tabasco was not put into the contraption by her husband and that the stagehand heard her speaking—proving that she was perfectly fine—up until the moment the cage was pushed out onto the stage for all to see. This further reinforces the notion of the 'impossible crime.' But already I see a problem. What if you are lying?"

He pointed at the stagehand.

"About what?"

"What if you did not hear her during those minutes? What if you killed her?"

"Nope," he said. "These two guys heard her, too."

"Indeed."

"Better watch what you say, buddy," one of the men said. "We're in the union."

Santorini, who had led us this far with some competence, began to falter. He was right about the basic facts. There was no ready explanation for what had happened to Kitty. As the hotel detective with the carnation and the ugly suit surmised, a thousand sets of eyes had not seen anyone kill Kitty Tabasco, and her husband could not have plunged the knife into her back. Moreover, I was the closest being to the victim, having been separated from her by only a thin piece of flooring and a few feet. And yet I had heard and seen nothing. All we knew was that Kitty had appeared in full view of everyone with a dagger in her back and already dead.

"What does it matter?" Tabasco said. "She's gone. She's at peace with the universe."

"It matters, sir," Captain Bostitch said, "because I will not have an unsolved murder on my ship. We have solved the suicide. There never was one. But the murder is a blight, sir. At peace? Believe that if you like. But I will not be at peace until this is made sense of."

Then Bostitch turned to Santorini. "Is there anything else?" he asked. "Anyone we can throw into the brig with hopes of a confession forthcoming?"

"I'm afraid not, Captain."

"What about these stagehands?" Captain Bostitch asked. "Pretty suspicious lot if you ask me. Could it be a conspiracy?"

"I don't think so."

Zest raised her hand as if she were in a classroom. "All of the evidence should be preserved for the forensics departments either in our next port of call or in the United States, isn't that right?"

"The corpse is going into cold storage along with all the other meat," Captain Bostitch said.

"Oh."

"Does anyone have anything to add?" Santorini asked. "As we go forward in this investigation I trust that you will all cooperate. I will most likely want to interview each of you individually to paint as full a picture of this sad event as possible."

"Are we done then?"

"For tonight, yes," Santorini said. "But I have to warn you that it must be assumed that whoever did this to poor Kitty is free aboard this ship and could strike again. And, Captain, please have those cages pushed to the side of the stage and unused for the duration of our journey. They also may contain important information. Does anyone have any questions?"

Captain Bostitch did. "There isn't anybody we can throw into the brig?"

"I'm afraid not."

"No one at all? Surely you suspect someone?"

"At this point, I suspect everyone."

"Well, that's a start. Narrow the list down a bit and I'll start throwing people in the brig."

"I'll keep you posted."

Zest offered to escort Tabasco to his suite, but he refused.

"No more cameras," he said.

Instead the cruise director, Melody Buttermold, arrived, having laid down her clipboard for the moment to take care of Tabasco. She also implored the captain to avoid passenger panic by suggesting that what the audience saw was not what they saw.

"I shall not lie," Captain Bostitch said.

"Not lie," Miss Buttermold said. "Just spin reality as positively as possible. After all, with the storm passed, tomorrow will be full of sunny-day activities and then we reach Curaçao."

Captain Bostitch sighed once again, reminded of what he did for a living.

"And don't forget the midnight buffet, everyone," Miss Buttermold chirped as she led Tabasco away. "Because of the bad weather we've just gotten through, the chefs are going to make tonight a real extravaganza. Don't miss it."

This did little to raise my spirits, since I was only too aware of the pink diet-restricting monstrosity around my neck. I soldiered on. While my owner and the others made plans, I retrieved a deep snout sample from the seat Tabasco had occupied during Santorini's disquisition.

This time I was surprised at what I found.

I DIDN'T HAVE LONG TO RE-
flect on my discovery or even assess it
properly, because Harry was calling my
name.

"Come on, Randolph," he said. Zest, Ivan Manners,
and Mr. Apples waited in the doorway of the theater.
"Hurry up, we're starving."

The dining room was filled with passengers, but for
some reason even though I had visited the space many
times before I had never really comprehended its sig-
nificance. Now at midnight, with the lights making all
of the stainless steel and the orange and red modular
table arrangements explode into vibrancy, I recognized
the Valhalla Vista for what it was: a temple to food. This
was not just a hungry dog's assessment.

The theater we had just left might have been grand,
but Valhalla Vista throbbed with life and mission. The
engine room propelled our craft forward, but this place
was the true center of the ship. Yes, there were dozens
of bars and other restaurants, but it was here that the

passengers, emerging from various states of gastric distress and biological terror, came to reveal the true purpose of their trip. There could be no question about it. The cruise ship existed and the southward journey was being taken to feed and further fatten these substantial passengers.

Even as one who enjoys the gifts of the stomach, this seemed too much to me. I began to feel a creeping, nihilistic terror as I watched all these people, giant paunches swelling oversized shirts, denim shorts plumped to bursting, fingers engorged like tubers, consuming heaping plates of food. I felt as I would at a witches' coven witnessing unnatural acts of rapacity and twisted appetite in the flickering light of a bonfire.

I told myself that I was being too harsh, but watching the single-minded purpose and the shoveling forks and the grinding jaws, I thought, *Is that all there is to this life—futile consumption of various combinations of chemicals to delight the neurons?* Maybe Jock Johnson was my unlikely savior and had pushed me through to the other side, to the life of detachment and the higher mind through sensory deprivation. I was free, I decided. Randolph would no longer be a slave to his appetites.

Just as I reached the mountaintop, Harry knelt down in front of me.

"See that?" he asked. My owner was pointing at seven clear plastic boxes along the wall. It was a buffet for dogs. The dogs, not trusted with self-directed sampling, were led along and stopped at whatever box contained food that they wanted. The owners would then scoop out a healthy spoonful onto a plate. Most dogs stopped at each box; some pawed frantically and received seconds. Then the plates were placed down on the floor and the contents hoovered up by Chihuahua and Great Dane alike.

I looked on with a newfound disgust at this spectacle.

Then Harry reached out and removed the pink monstrosity from my collar.

"To hell with Jock Johnson," he said. "It's been a hard night."

There was sausage, ham, steak, and eggs. There were bacon-flavored patties. There were waffles. I had seconds, thirds, and fourths. I ate without a sense of time or self. I was all stomach and in the spell of the ecstatic worship of the Delicious. All that was left of my high principle was embedded in my whiskers with the other remnants of my dinner.

"Are you breathing?" Harry asked, leaning over me. I was on my back beneath a table, giving room to my generous belly and trying to focus on a point on the ceiling.

"Is he all right?" I heard Zest ask. All I could see was her legs in bright pink stockings festooned with anchors.

"He's been on a diet," Harry explained.

"He'll need to go on another one," she said.

There were other legs at the table. Ivan's and

another pair I could not identify. The rush of blood sugar made my head spin. Slowly, I drifted back down to the floor and realized that precious minutes had passed and the people above me at the table were discussing Kitty Tabasco.

I rolled onto my belly and pushed up onto my paws. People were still crowding the buffet line and shoveling delectables into their maws, but I looked at them differently now. I had returned to my level. I was one with them, bound to this earth by the gravity of my own appetites. No dog should ever get haughty. It isn't good for the soul.

I sat on my haunches and surveyed the table. The pair of alien legs belonged to Frank Booker, the car salesman from Pasadena turned tractor salesman from Brattleboro, Vermont. He was devouring lobster tortellini in a vodka cream sauce and listening to Zest hold forth on the events of the night. This immediately set me on my guard even though, as before, I could smell no sinister intent.

"This cruise just gets better and better," Zest said as she placed a second broccoli spear in her mouth and chewed the fat-free lemon-drenched butterless green that would not add an ounce to her whippet-thin video-friendly body.

Frank Booker interrupted her.

"Is that all you're gonna eat?"

"It is very satisfying," Zest said as if trying to convince herself. "The key is quality not quantity. Did you know that people in famines are actually healthier on average than people who are not in famines? I did a story on it for Channel Eight. We flew to Africa. I got to wear a safari hat and khakis from Urbane Outfitters. The poor starving people thought I was a goddess. It took so much to convince them otherwise. I showed them my tattoo—the one I got in Cancun during college. I'll never drink like that again."

"So starving people actually live longer than people who are not starving?" Booker asked, mopping up the last of his vodka cream sauce with a cranberry walnut muffin. His plate was littered with the remains of foods that only a buffet of the scope of the *Nordic Bliss*'s would ever allow assembled on a single plate.

"Well, not those people in Africa, but the average starving person like someone in Miami or LA. Of course, it helps if you smoke. And I just love broccoli. Anyway, you interrupted me. I was talking about our cruise. I mean, we've just landed in the middle of a major news event and there's absolutely no one here to cover it except me. I am so totally excited. It's like I've woken up and it's Christmas and my birthday all at once."

"Shame about Kitty," Harry muttered, but nothing could check Zest's enthusiasm for telegenic tragedy.

"Do you think there's going to be anyone else?" Booker asked.

"I hope so," Zest said and then, perhaps hearing how that sounded, caught herself. "You know what I mean. It's natural for a journalist to feel that way because it would add to the story. You want it but you don't want it at the same time. Obviously, for the victim it's a shame."

"I'm not sure about you journalist types," Booker said.

"The thing is someone's got to get this story, and my team is here to report it."

"Did you get footage of the murder?" Harry asked.

"My guy's reviewing the rushes again right now, but from what he said and what I saw all we've got is the prep for the trick, you and the dog up on the stage, cages being spun, curtains being dropped then lifted, and Kitty dead with the knife in her back. It's dramatic and all, but from a law enforcement perspective it's worthless."

Zest began to eat a small custard tart that she told everyone at the table she had "earned."

"But in a way, as much as I like doing it, news reporting is basically dead. By the time we get to port, this whole story is going to be all over the world and even if I do a stand-up or two, that'll be it for the news portion of the story. In other words, from a career perspective there's no real benefit. I'll still be covering kids, animals, and street fairs when I get back to New York. But there's something I can do, something longer and something that I can sell nationwide. I was going to do this with the Tabasco profile but now the story's even bigger. I want to solve this case."

"How are you going to do that?" Ivan asked.

"You and Harry are going to help me. The key isn't actually solving it," Zest explained. "For television it just means making the story of trying to solve it as dramatically interesting as possible. I can think of a dozen channels that would scoop this up. I mean, think about what and who we've got."

The custard tart was gone and Zest helped herself to a portion of a cherry-cheese Danish from Ivan's plate without seeming to notice what she was doing.

"First, we've got a very well-known main character, Milton Tabasco. We've got marital strife, romantic love, and tragedy with Kitty Tabasco. We've got murder. We've got an investigator, that cheesy hotel detective Santorini. And we've got two paranormal investigators, a parrot, and a dog. This is better than Hollywood. It's real life."

"So what are you proposing?" Ivan asked.

"I'm saying that over the next two days we do three things: First, we follow Santorini as he investigates the crime; then we keep following Tabasco, leaving our options of his portrayal open because he's either a victim or the perp; and finally we keep you two involved doing the paranormal stuff since there are big audiences for it, and if nothing happens on the criminal investigation side I'll have the hocus-pocus stuff to fall back on to fill in potential dead air."

"It's not hocus-pocus," Ivan said.

"You know what I mean," Zest said. "So are you two

in? I mean, this could be the opportunity of a lifetime, Ivan. Both of us should be thinking national."

"It's a great idea," Ivan declared. "But only if you promise that some of my own infrared video shooting will be used to highlight ectoplasmic events."

"I can't promise anything," Zest said.

"How about billing me as a renowned international ghost hunter?"

"That I can do," Zest said.

"I'm going to pass," Harry said.

"That's fine," Ivan said.

"That's not fine," Zest snapped. "I'm not interested in you unless Harry's part of the deal, too."

"Harry," Ivan implored. "Do it for me, and if that's not enough do it for the future of ghost science. If we can prove something on national television, it's going to shatter some beliefs."

"It's not my thing," Harry said.

As much as I disliked the thought of either Harry or myself appearing on national television, I knew that Zest's plan was critical to determining Kitty Tabasco's killer and possibly even protecting Harry and myself. Something about the way Frank Booker shifted in his seat while Zest spoke and a certain scent of hostility made me think that Booker didn't like the idea of Harry being busy and presumably surrounded by people for the duration of the cruise.

It was time to offer my counsel by giving a jog to my owner's memory. I rested my chin on his leg.

"Randolph, not now," Harry said.

I lifted my paw. This was one of those insufferably "cute" canine behaviors I never did.

"Randolph wants you to do it," Zest said. Her words seemed to trigger something in Harry. Was it the memory of Holmes's video telegram? He looked at me with that discomforting expression that I had seen before, as if he were about to recognize that his animal was sentient, a fellow traveler on the road of a conscious life. Fortunately, I overestimated.

"He's your dog if you want someone to drool over witnesses," Harry said.

"And you're my man if I want to give the female demographic someone to drool over. Please help make this happen," Zest said. I could smell that the ambitious television reporter had not given up on her goal of corralling my owner. Yet I would have to take the risk of her proximity to Harry. I put my other paw up so that I was now hanging from his leg. It seemed impossible that even my easily distracted and impressionistic owner would forget Holmes's instructions that I was inspired.

"Okay, I'll do it," Harry said.

"I'm so happy," Zest said.

She polished off Ivan's cherry-cheese Danish as she went over some of the more gripping aspects of recent events.

"You couldn't ask for a better television detective than this guy Santorini. I mean, he's almost too good to be true. You heard him, we've got an 'impossible crime' on our hands. This is a murder that shouldn't have happened, but did. Very exciting."

"Did you say 'impossible crime'?" Frank Booker asked. He had left the table for a while during the negotiations with Harry and seemed a little stung at not being asked to join Zest's video project. "It sounds like the killer's a mystery buff."

"Why do you say that?"

"Only a mystery buff would care about committing an 'impossible crime.' It's too elegant for the average murderer and too complicated. Why go to all that trouble? Also, it's obvious that the one person who didn't do it is Milton Tabasco."

"Why's that?" Zest asked.

"Because he's the guy everyone's going to think did it. I read a lot of classic mysteries. In the 'impossible crime' category, the impossibility of the thing almost always means that the killer's never who you expect it to be. The killer's more likely to be Captain Bostitch than Milton Tabasco. Who knows? Maybe Kitty Tabasco killed herself."

"With a knife in the middle of her back?"

"There are ways," Booker said as if he knew such things better than the average man.

"Well, I'm off, boys," Zest said. She wanted to start early and arranged to meet Ivan and Harry at eight the next morning in the café near the ship's gym.

"They've got steel-cut oatmeal to die for," she said.

Frank Booker departed next, leaving Harry and Ivan alone.

"I didn't tell you something," Harry said.

"What's that?"

"I got a message from the other side. A spirit guide called Holmes. He's communicated with me before. He said that he inspired Randolph."

I couldn't believe what Harry was revealing. Hadn't I been clear in my instructions that my owner should tell no one?

"How did he communicate?"

"Through the ship's video telegram," Harry said. "In the past it was by arranging Alpha-Bits cereal."

"Are you joking?"

"No," Harry said. "What's so surprising? Hasn't that happened to you?"

"Hardly," Ivan said. "Even the best spiritualists don't get definitive stuff like that—usually they can't rule out their subconscious playing tricks on them. The cereal writing falls into that category. But a video telegram? Wow. That's a whole different story. I've got to see that message."

"It's back in my room."

"Let's go."

"Right now?"

"Harry, don't you see how important this is? I mean you got a supernatural communication through an electronic medium. This message is traceable. We can see where on the ship it came from. We can find a trail. To

my knowledge there is no record of electronic corre-
spondence from the other side, ever."

The two men rose.

"I don't care about that as much as what it said."

"What did it say?"

"That Milton Tabasco had something to do with his
wife's death."

"What's wrong with that?"

"The message came while Kitty was alive, after she
had supposedly jumped overboard but before tonight
when she actually died. How can a spirit observer be
wrong?"

"I wouldn't worry about it. Their sense of time isn't
the same on the other side. And besides, your spirit basically got it right. She's dead now, isn't she?"

The dining area had emptied. I was the only dog
left, and Harry and Ivan were among the only human
passengers. A squad of Scandinavians were scrubbing
the floors. I watched with mixed emotions as the dog
buffet disappeared through the double doors into the
kitchen. We walked on the open deck for part of the
way back to our cabin. Tonight was much like the first
night of the cruise, except the air was much warmer. It
was no longer oppressive as it had been during the
storm, but there was a stable kind of heat that made
you aware that we were nearing the equator.

Ivan talked on and on about the momentousness of
the video telegram for the ghost-hunting world. Harry
listened but suggested that as per usual there would be

no way to prove it. He also, I was relieved to note, did not reveal to Ivan that I was supposed to be spiritually "inspired." The last thing I wanted was Ivan taking a special interest in me. Mr. Apples was vaguely perceived as a spiritual being by Ivan, but a verifiable animal envoy for the other side would get his complete attention.

Fortunately, circumstances intervened. When we reached the bowels of the ship, it was clear that the coeds had recovered and were back to their hard drinking entertainment. The quilters were silent.

We reached our cabin and Harry was about to insert his electronic card key when he saw that the door was already unlocked and, in fact, slightly ajar.

"I must have forgotten to close it," he said as he pushed the door into the room.

But when he flicked on the light, it was immediately clear that it was not Harry's oversight. Our little room had been ransacked, to the extent that this was even possible since we had brought so few possessions with us. The mattress had been turned over and with apparent brutality sliced open at the top where Harry's head went. The sheets that had been on the mattress had been thrown onto the floor along with the towels and all of Harry's clothes. The desk drawers had been removed and dumped. One had been broken in half. Harry's suitcase had had all of its external pockets sliced open and its contents dumped onto the floor as well. Even the pillow had been cut open. Feathers covered the room.

"Oh, no," Harry said.

I tried to snuffle around to get some kind of scent, but Harry stopped me.

"Out, Randolph," he said and edged me into the hallway where I remained listening to my owner thud about our distressed cabin while Ivan commented.

"They were obviously looking for something," Ivan said. "They weren't thieves or they would have taken that money on the dresser."

Harry let out an epithet when he examined the bathroom.

"Did they have to dump everything on the floor?"

"I told you, they were looking for something," Ivan said. "What were you hiding?"

"Absolutely nothing."

"They didn't think so," Ivan said. "I guess you have some enemies, my friend."

Harry considered dialing ship security but decided against it when he realized that Santorini might show up and spend half an hour describing what literary mystery precedent had just been observed. Adding to my owner's distress was the fact that when he tried to show Ivan my video telegram, the communications system reported that it had been deleted.

Ivan yawned and begged off to bed, leaving Harry with the task of making some sense of his room.

"I'll call security tomorrow when I have the

strength to deal with whoever they send," he said to me, having let me back in the room and instructed me to sit in a corner. I took deep snoutfuls of air in an attempt to determine any distinct smell that might help me identify the person or persons who had done this, but all I came up with was a slick, metallic cologne. At first I thought this would make for an easy identification— until I recognized where I had smelled this before. It was standard issue scent for the crew members of the *Nordic Bliss* and so potent that it obliterated any underlying scents. Most perfumes and colognes blend with a person's skin to make a distinct fragrance, but this one only made everyone smell like everyone else.

Harry heaved the mattress off the floor and turned it over so that the slit faced down. He resheeted the bed and retrieved a new pillow from the closet in the hall to replace the one that had been split open. He left most of the feathers alone, but in the spot that had been designated for my sleep my owner knelt down and brushed the area clean with his hands. It was a kind gesture and one that reminded me that as reckless and dangerously abstract as my owner could sometimes seem, those behaviors were beyond his control, and the damage he did was not out of willful choice. He paused in his work but stayed on one knee. He seemed momentarily overcome by this intrusion into our space. It was painful to see because I sensed all of his pent-up longing for Imogen and his fear that we would never reach her. For the third time that evening, I rested my paw on his leg. And for the first time that evening, he gave me a pat.

"You're such a good dog," Harry said. "I wouldn't have gotten this far without you."

Then he stood up and wedged a piece of the broken drawer into the seam beneath the door to act as a jamb in case someone tried to get in again during the night.

Harry lay down on the bed and I curled up on the floor. He turned the television to the nautical information channel and within minutes I had drowsed off to the image of our ship's bow plowing through placid southern seas and the digital display of our steady speed.

A DOG GOES POOLSIDE

CURIOUS COMPULSIONS EMERGE

"IS EVERYONE READY TO have their glands expressed?" a woman wearing a bright pink leotard screamed at an assembled crowd of dogs and their humans.

I for one was not ready to have my glands expressed, examined, or tampered with. Fortunately, a dozen corgis had been recruited for the job. She was pointing at them now and gesturing to a long strip of bright white carpet. I was staying safely out of reach in the back row.

I had awoken with the televised dawn light playing across my eyelids and the old circadian rhythms making my stomach grumble for more food despite the previous night's gorge. The sun had broken the horizon to the left of the screen, and there wasn't a cloud in the sky. Tropical Storm Sedadog™ was far away. At first I had been glad for the promise of a normal day, but that was before we had gotten on deck.

Harry and our little group were eager to continue investigations, but the good weather and the determined Miss Buttermold had conspired to turn Deck 12 into a dog free-for-all. The cruise director now had to accommodate all of the people whose exhibits, demonstrations, booths, and lectures had been canceled during the storm. Her solution was to cram as many of them into the schedule as possible.

In an effort to weave through heavy foot traffic, my owner and I had been stranded in a corner of the Poop Deck with the pink leotard gland lady. She was now describing the glands in question to an assembled crowd.

"You see, dogs have two big sacs right inside their rectums that carry their own customized scent. Most of the time these glands function just fine. Usually when your dear ones go potty, these glands empty. But sometimes they don't."

Despite the clamor from other events right around us, the gland lady spoke with such compelling force that even the corgis tilted their heads to listen.

"And when they don't empty," she said, "their little bottoms itch. And when they itch, our little darlings scratch the only way they know how. They scoot. You've all seen it. Cringe-inducing, right? When your little darlings decide to scoot over your carpet?"

Heads nodded. Even the corgis seemed to agree that scooting was "cringe-inducing."

"Sometimes the problem is easily alleviated by weight loss," she said looking directly at me. "Our heavyset friends have difficulty emptying their sacs. A vet or a groomer can offer a short-term solution. But weight loss is the best long-term solution."

The gland lady and the attentive corgis were, I realized, part of the sales effort.

"So let's take it to the carpet. This carpet," she said. "The purpose of today's demonstration is to show everyone the power of the *Canine Crusader*. This vacuum cleaner brought to you by the world's greatest engineers combines the power of an agricultural harvester with the precision of a laser dental drill to create an end-user experience that is utterly flawless. You have never and will never encounter another vacuum cleaner that literally rips the dirt, mold, grime, and yuckiness right out of a carpet and restores it to its original state. Now let's do some scooting."

The corgis snapped to attention, and then with what must have instantly ranked as one of the most humiliating dog episodes in the service of man, they began to "scoot" one after the other across the pristine carpet, dragging their petite rears in jerky motion behind them. I turned away in disgust and acute embarrassment for my kind.

"Look at them go," exclaimed the gland lady. "In case you're wondering, they're racing because the fastest one gets the best treat."

Sure enough, the fastest corgi found himself chewing on two biscuits while his compatriots had to settle for one. Their scooting had resulted in a soiled carpet onto which, in classic sales fashion, the lady dumped every kind of grotesque substance possible and then defied the audience to imagine the carpet coming clean again. She used an average vacuum cleaner to predictably poor results and then turned to the *Canine Crusader,* a stainless-steel canister on tank treads with two attack dogs emblazoned on its flanks. When the machine was turned on it sounded like a bear emitting a continuous growl at the back of a cave. As the *Canine Crusader* glided over the mess, the mess began to disappear.

"Amazing," she exclaimed. But it was a tough crowd, most of whom were only sticking around because, like Harry and myself, they were stuck in traffic. The gland lady began to grow desperate.

"I forgot the hair," she said. "What it does with hair is absolutely phenomenal—by the way, everyone, if your dog is losing too much hair it might be a vitamin deficiency, so check with your vet. Where's that hair?"

She picked up a bucket of dog hair and began to sprinkle it in front of the *Canine Crusader.* A ball hidden in the bucket dropped onto the carpet as well. Unfortunately, the ball was a favorite of one of the corgis, who went after it. The efficient machine devoured the hair, the ball, and the corgi with a whump whump whump and a whimper (the distinctive corgi whimper that has been likened by corgi authorities to the whistle of a high-end teakettle).

"This is not ideal," the gland lady observed as the crowd gaped in shock. "They're rentals."

She switched the *Canine Crusader* off and turned the machine on its side.

"Now, there's no reason to worry because the *Canine Crusader* has no teeth, rotating brushes, or moving parts—just tornado-like suction. Moonbeam will be just fine."

She was right. Moonbeam was rumpled but intact and the gland lady continued on with the demonstration, ratcheting up the level of difficulty by staining the rug with grape juice, muesli, coffee, and more dog fur. Desperation was evident and the *Canine Crusader* insatiable, so when the foot traffic lightened, Harry and I quickly moved past the spectacle and the increasingly hysterical pitch of the gland lady, who was now emptying a huge bag of concrete powder.

But evidence of the market for dog-related goods and services was everywhere. The celebrity chef was cooking "high-value" crêpes for dogs and telling her audience that a dog without a crêpe in his bowl had a three times greater likelihood of suffering from stomach-related depression than his crêpe-fed counterpart. We walked on past dogs wearing blinders for undisturbed REM sleep, dogs wearing "white noise" earphones for the calming of nerves, dogs wearing boots for the easing of something called canine quadrupedal disorder—which from what I could gather was sore feet—and finally a contingent of canines wearing T-shirts that I found eerily familiar.

Why familiar? Because emblazoned across the backs of my small brethren were identifiers coined (I had thought) by Yours Truly. A dachshund's shirt proclaimed him A SQUAT-AND-DROP; a Chihuahua was A ZIGZAG DUMPER; a terrier, A FOLIAGE FINDER. Here in black-and-white (and sometimes color) print were my own words. This was my shorthand to describe the bathroom habits and temperaments of my kind as observed at New York City's dog runs, and yet I had never expressed my labels beyond the confines of my own mind. How was this possible? How could someone be making money from my thoughts? It was a big world with many creative brains dwelling on the universe's quirks, but still...

I didn't have time to explore this mystery, because Zest had appeared with her camera crew and Ivan in tow.

"Harry, where have you been?" Zest asked. "Santorini's over at the pool with Tabasco. Tabasco's doing a demonstration showing how dogs can be cured of their fears by being exposed to them. We need your dog."

"Why?"

"He's got to be in these shots," Zest said. "It'll establish him as a character for the audience."

I didn't want to be established as a character for anyone, but proximity to Tabasco and Santorini was welcome. We hurried to the pool, Zest barreling ahead and wedging the crowd apart like a force of nature. Harry had no time to mention that our room had been ransacked the night before and question what, if anything, this had to do with Kitty's demise and our current investigation. I bobbed along behind the humans, powered on half a handful of the meager purple foodstuff and the memory of last night's dinner.

The pool offered a different kind of spectacle. Here the selling was not so explicit. Milton Tabasco was once removed from crass commercialism by being busy in telegraphing his so-called dog philosophy. His odd, impromptu language was but one part of his approach, and now at the pool he reveled in the physical component of the Dog Mutterer way.

He stood at the deep end of the pool. The deck was crowded with owners and their dogs. Deck chairs and chaise lounges had been piled in the corners to make more room for his audience. We arrived to a deep and respectful silence. Zest's crew began immediately filming while the reporter, Harry, Ivan, and I remained on the outside of the crowd. We had come from the aft of the ship and were fortunate to have a view because the pool and surrounding deck were at the base of a flight of steps several feet below where we stood. Santorini, seeming in the light of a near-Caribbean morning to be even more absurd and unlikely than he had been at the theater, stood on the opposite side of the pool area and had Tabasco fixed in a melodramatic glare.

"Animals, as you all know, are fear-based creatures," Tabasco was saying. "To understand animals, you must understand that unlike us, they are much closer to raw fear. Have you ever awoken in the middle of the night and been terrified of something but not known what it was? Has anyone here ever suffered a panic attack?"

A few hands went up.

"Then you'll understand what I'm talking about," Tabasco continued. "A dog is a heartbeat away from a panic attack from the moment it is born until the moment it dies. I know that sometimes it doesn't seem that way, but believe me it's true. Dogs are afraid because nature's scary, and just because they're living in man's world doesn't mean they get over their fear."

Tabasco was holding a medium-sized dog that looked like a cross between a Scotty and a Labrador. He was stroking the dog under its chin; its legs hung straight down, totally relaxed.

"He looks calm, doesn't he?" Tabasco said. "Well, he isn't."

Tabasco jerked his hand slightly, and the dog immediately froze.

"Fear," he said. "Fear at the slightest hint of trouble."

He began walking toward a device that looked like a catapult. In fact, it was a catapult.

"In recent years we've learned a lot about the brain, and one thing we've learned is that exposure to the object of fear can actually build up a kind of 'immunity' to fear. In other words, we can burn out those parts of the brain that cause fear by triggering them over and over again. Now, my gut instincts told me this long before the science caught up, and that's why I developed this method."

Tabasco put the dog down in the basket of the catapult. The dog looked up at Tabasco with a distinct look of terror in his eyes, a kind of desperation and helplessness as if he knew what was coming next but could do nothing about it. He tried to escape the basket, but Tabasco did some focused Muttering and the dog froze.

"Now, Tolstoy's done this drill before," he said. "Haven't you, Tolstoy? He hasn't quite gotten to burnout level yet. But he will…"

Tabasco pushed a foot lever and the catapult sprung. Tolstoy went flying through the air with a yelp and into the pool. He did not look happy. After furiously paddling to the edge he pulled himself out and shook.

"A big hand for Tolstoy," Tabasco said. He commanded Tolstoy to return with some more copyrighted dog speech and the dog was soon sitting in the basket once again, awaiting another launch.

"What's happening in Tolstoy's brain is called reprogramming," Tabasco said. "Somehow Tolstoy developed a fear of being in the air. This fear is the direct result of losing control. A very common condition among dogs. Rather than juice the guy up on meds, I'm a big believer in exposing him to as much stress as possible until he basically breaks and simply can't bear feeling scared anymore. And when a dog can't bear feeling scared anymore, he stops feeling scared. Isn't that right, Tolstoy?"

Tabasco released the catapult again.

"Lift off," he said, watching Tolstoy repeat the journey. "Eventually, Tolstoy will be cured. It might not happen today, but it will happen soon. The same can be true of any dog for almost any problem. Since fear is always at the bottom, exhausting that fear is the solution. Another huge fear is thunder . . ."

This time Tolstoy was put into Tabasco's thunder machine and subjected to a simulation of an electric storm during which he cowered and bayed but eventually showed signs of calming down.

"I've been told my methods are cruel," Tabasco said. "But that's envy, folks. Who else gets a one hundred percent cure rate for these conditions? And no medicine with its toxic side effects. This is about harnessing the power of the brain to heal itself."

Some people applauded, but a few passengers, clearly upset by the Tabasco method, harrumphed and stalked off.

"Do we have any volunteers? Any dogs with acute fears that you want the Dog Mutterer to personally cure?" Two dozen hands went up and two dozen sets of canine eyes belonging to these hands looked anxiously

on. Apparently, Tabasco was unsatisfied with this seemingly robust interest.

"Folks, rich people pay me thousands of bucks to do
this and I'm offering it to you for free."

A dozen more hands were thrust into the air.

Someone sharply nudged my hindquarters. Zest had
her hand up and was forcing me forward down the
steps. Once again the Dog Mutterer selected me for his
demonstration. My empty stomach was twisted into
knots but I moved forward, anxious to put myself in
Tabasco's scent circle.

"Wait a minute," Harry blurted out, but it was too
late. The crowd closed in behind us, blocking my owner
from following, and already I was beside Tabasco.

"You're becoming a regular, aren't you?" he said.
"Into the catapult."

I obliged. Zest stood next to me with a reportorial
agenda ready to be inflicted on the Dog Mutterer. His
foot crept to the release button.

"Kitty invented this method, didn't she?" Zest
asked. I could see that she was miked and her cameraman was standing only a few feet away.

Tabasco looked mournful.

"Oh, yes," he said. "She was the genius on our team.
I knew dogs feared. She knew how to make them fear
less."

This method didn't seem to be working on me, because as he talked I began to want very much to get
out of the basket. In an effort to distract myself, I

snout-stamped the Dog Mutterer to get a thorough and
updated scent. There was an overlay of sadness and also
one of romantic longing. (This is what had surprised
me the night before.) Was it for Kitty? I didn't think so,
because unlike the night before he now emitted a distinct lavender scent that was likely the scent of whoever it was he longed for. There was also resentment
at Zest's inquiry even though he seemed receptive on
the surface. In fact, there was more than resentment:
There was fear and nervousness. It was the fear and
nervousness of someone who did not want to be found
out.

"It must be hard to have lost Kitty twice," Zest continued.

"Oh, God, yes," Tabasco said and tried to end the inquiry by triggering the catapult. I closed my eyes and
gritted my jaws, but I did not go flying. Instead the catapult lifted a foot or so in the air, and then with a crack
the arm split in two and dropped the basket down to its
original position. Everyone laughed at the fat dog who
had just broken the device and ruined the demonstration. Everyone, that is, except for Harry and Milton
Tabasco, who reached down and with a genuine ear rub
and head pat told me it was okay.

I hopped out of the basket and sought anonymity,
but it was not to be. Melody Buttermold arrived and announced that the dog "triathlon" was about to begin.
Dogs and their human companions would compete in a
three-part event that would take them from a log roll in

the swimming pool, to the climbing wall, to a "food" obstacle course set up on the volleyball courts that would test a dog's discipline. The winner would be awarded a shiny trophy and a year's supply of the monks' grooming products, which included an avocado-based ear cleaner and a lanolin snout moisturizer. The only condition was that the Dog Mutterer himself would be competing with an animal of his choice against all comers.

"This has got to be filmed," Zest said. "And you have *got* to use Randolph."

Tabasco looked down at me doubtfully. "He doesn't look like a triathlete."

"With you leading the way, I'm sure he'll do fine."

"These are serious athletic challenges."

I heartily shared his doubts about my competence. If interpreting Dante was the job, or waxing wide on the nature of dog–man relations or the philosophical problems of good and evil, there would be no question that I was the dog. But physical exertion was not a strength.

"That fat is really just muscle in training," Zest said. "And it will make you look so adorable helping a loser."

This was unnecessary, but the public relations aspect apparently appealed to Tabasco. We became a team.

Dogs and their owners lined up in front of Melody Buttermold, who was taking names and giving out waterproof bands to be worn around legs or tails. I was

Number 8. The "log" roll consisted of a narrow plastic cylinder that ran the entire width of the pool. This being the largest pool on the ship, the log was quite long. It was also slick and rotated with the slightest bit of force. One of the Scandinavians tested it and fell into the water before he got halfway across. They tightened something so it didn't spin as quickly. Still, the second time he tested it he only got three-quarters of the way.

Fortunately for the canine competitors, we did not have to worry about crossing the pool, only staying in one place longer than our adversaries on the other end. There were ten teams comprising all shapes, sizes, and breeds, and Miss Buttermold had waived all pretense of fairness in the matchups. The first one saw a three-hundred-pound man and a dachshund against a child and a sheepdog. All four were dunked simultaneously. Watching the spectacle, the whoops and frivolity of the crowd, the almost hungry aspect of the audience— I had seen such things on television but never in person—I began to feel very nervous. There was something barbaric about it even if it was all being done in bright colors and underneath the hot sun. The next two matches were just as short-lived as the first, and the fourth ended in default when one competitor, a Pomeranian named Duffy, refused to walk out onto the log and was disqualified. Tabasco and I went last.

The Dog Mutterer began with his usual beguil-

ing set of commands. "Broccoli . . . spare tire . . . flabber-
gast . . . mixed up . . . hobo . . . cosmic masterpiece . . ."

The barrage had its usual hypnotic effect. I found
myself getting to my paws and following him to our side
of the pool. Our adversaries were already preparing to
step out onto the log. Miss Buttermold held a stopwatch and motioned us to get to our starting block,
from which we would step out onto the water. To prevent the log from rolling prematurely, two Scandinavians stood chest-deep in the water keeping it steady.

The crowd started screaming wildly when Tabasco,
who had made a costume change and now wore a Dog
Mutterer sweat suit with matching sweatband, ac-
knowledged the crowd with big waves and slapped the
backs and pinched the cheeks of those directly surrounding us.

Our competition waited on the other side of the
pool: a Chihuahua the size of a hamster and her ballerina owner. The situation was not promising. I am top-
heavy and, besides, Labradors do not like standing on
anything but terra firma. Tabasco was a large man with
wide shoulders. I was certain we were headed for the
drink.

"Matterhorn . . . latchkey . . . kaboom . . . ," Tabasco
said leading the way onto the log. I found myself following him out above the water.

Then Miss Buttermold blew her whistle, the Scandinavians released their grip on the log, and it began to

slowly rotate. It rotated left. It rotated right. It rotated left again.

The ballerina shouted commands at her dog.

"To the right Dame Judith...bow, Dame Judith... to the left...to the left...to the left."

Milton Tabasco spoke in Dog Mutter. "Kitchner... dubious...Macanudo...lavatory..."

"Five seconds," Miss Buttermold announced.

The log grew more unstable, its jerks right and left more sudden and unpredictable.

"Ten seconds," Miss Buttermold said. "Fifteen seconds is the time to beat."

Another second ticked by, and then another. Somehow I was staying on the log and out of the pool.

Another second. The crowd roared.

"Fifteen seconds," Miss Buttermold yelled. "One or the other of these two teams will win this segment."

"Literal...bang bang...fatty fat fat...stay on, you bastard," instructed Tabasco. Our opponent human actually pirouetted, and Dame Judith knelt. They were supremely confident; I, however, was losing my balance. And then Tabasco jumped straight up and landed with such force that he put the log into a tremendous spin. This should have finished us. I felt myself falling toward the water, but just as this was happening I did a sort of split and instead of tipping over I landed straight down on the log, straddling it. The log spun beneath me with my legs hanging into the water on each side. This was humiliating and mildly painful though apparently legal. Tabasco stayed atop the log as well, but our opponents did not. Dame Judith and her ballerina toppled into the water.

"Seventeen and a half seconds," Miss Buttermold exclaimed. "We have a winner."

I could have remained on the log indefinitely, but was scooped up by one of the attendant Scandinavians and placed poolside to several back rubs of congratulations. It took me a minute to recognize that the pink monstrosity around my neck had sustained terminal water damage (it was promptly removed and disposed of).

The competition continued at the climbing wall, where it was each human's task to hoist his or her canine charge up a studded ascent. The dog had to do his or her part by making a show of climbing and actually push up the near-vertical surface. This was a pointless challenge for most dogs, since they had no idea what was going on and either went totally limp or pushed off the wall, making it very hard for them to be lifted at all.

Tabasco and I went last. As I was being harnessed he bent down and instructed: "Cauliflower … steamroller … applesauce …"

And then in a softer voice that no one except me heard: "We both know how smart you are. I want to win and you'd better help me."

I didn't hesitate. Even though it was awkward to be

heaved skyward, I padded up the wall as if I were scampering through Central Park. We won easily with a mark of fifteen feet, eight inches.

"Smile for the camera, you two," Zest instructed as her cameraman went in for the close-up.

Next came the food-based obstacle course held on the volleyball court. The final battle. The purpose of this was to test in a very obvious way the control that each owner had over his or her charge. Foods of every variety and kind were arrayed in a maze-like way and at every height to trap the small and large dog alike.

Again, Tabasco knelt down beside me.

"Your weakness is your stomach. You are going to resist this weakness or else."

Great air currents of delectables reached my nose: meats, fish, desserts of every kind. There were even *pigs in a blanket*. I wanted Tabasco to win because winning would keep us in closer proximity and closer proximity would mean that I would learn more.

Technically, according to Miss Buttermold, the team of Tabasco and Randolph could still lose if Randolph ate every single delectable and the dog in closest contention, Dame Judith, did not.

The other teams raced through the obstacle course. The Great Dane who had done miserably on the log and the climbing wall did miserably here as well, clearing several of the plates and forcing the Scandinavians to replenish with fresh food. Dame Judith did remarkably well and avoided all delectables but one, a single lobster puff on a pile of twenty.

Then it was our turn. My stomach was in full-scale revolt. I felt faint from the athletic exertion, and the aroma of each food gripped me. I had sudden flashes—hallucinations even—that I was eating without end and that it was perfectly fine to be eating. In fact, Tabasco was feeding me, shoveling the food into my mouth.

Except that he wasn't doing this at all, and I had demolished the contents of Obstacles 1, 2, and 3 in a kind of trance. Where Dame Judith had sampled a single lobster puff, I had taken the plate.

Tabasco glared at me as we approached Obstacle 4, a veal pâté with a delicate parsley garnish.

"Streetlight . . . Paris . . . birthday candle . . . wire your mouth shut . . ."

I was slipping in and out of conscious control. This maze of food was too strong for my lower natures. Obstacles 4, 5, and 6 vanished into my gullet. Tabasco was fuming publicly now. Miss Buttermold was announcing that the race was getting close. There was only one food left, and if I didn't resist this one all would be lost.

This last obstacle, unfortunately, was *pigs in a blanket*. I could see Harry standing in the crowd. Did I detect guilt at having allowed his dog to go through such humiliation and struggle? No, I don't think so. I could see what was almost hopefulness in his eyes—as if somehow I would win despite the odds. He knew my weaknesses and had often coddled them, but here he was extending belief in me. He was actually shouting my name. The Dog Mutterer was trying his hypnotic best to control my appetites, but in the end it was Harry's faith in his dog that put an end to my rampage. It wasn't easy, and the gravitational pull of those delectables was profound. They had been toasted to perfection and the hot dogs were dripping with grease, but I passed them by. I would not see their like again.

We had won. Zest told the cameraman to go in for a close-up. A shiny trophy and a year's supply of avocado-based ear cleaner and lanolin snout moisturizer were ours.

Being of a reflective and literary disposition, I had always considered winning and losing to be primitive states. The craving to be on top, the horror of being a failure seemed things that shouldn't concern someone who has moved beyond into the elevated heights of intellect and spirit. Poetry has no room for winners or losers; it only has room for those who are ready to sample the rich harvest of life's experience without categories and easy characterization. As a dog, I'm quick to see the animal-based territoriality and aggressiveness in winning and losing—how much of it probably gets back to our concerns about where the next meal is coming from or whether we'll be eaten by a tiger. At a New York City dog run, you see that there's not much distance between a poodle snapping at another dog because some invisible line has been crossed and the poodle's owner sitting on a bench nearby bellowing into a phone.

But this victory had changed things for me. I had always disparaged the life of action in favor of the life of books to be found in my cozy corner of Manhattan. But here I was a champion with a trophy and a yearlong supply of organic products, striding the deck being admired by others for my achievements. And these achievements were about doing something instead of merely thinking about something. The achievements were about taking action, black-and-white action in a very gray world.

All of this was doing wonders for my confidence until the laughter began. At first it was a mere ripple as I ascended a makeshift podium for the trophy presentation. But then the grinning, snickering, elbow nudging, and occasional guffaw grew into a torrent of collective hilarity. And just as I was having a ribbon draped about my neck by Miss Buttermold (Tabasco would carry the trophy), the pointing at my hindquarters began and to my horror I fell from the inflated heights of conquering hero to the depths of a dependent dog.

"What's that hanging from his ass?" blurted out one crude observer.

"They look like purple nuggets."

"Yuck," a child said. "They're doodies. Purple doodies."

And indeed they were purple doodies. My radical change in diet had led to intestinal disorder. Thanks to Jock Johnson and the shortcomings of my own canine delivery system, I was standing on the victor's podium with waste product dangling from my rear, stuck to its Velcro-like fur.

"Purple doodies," the child repeated, gripped by the music of the words. "Purple doodies. Purple doodies."

There was no foliage to find nor dark of night to hide my shame. I imagined Zest's cameraman going in for a close-up. Miss Buttermold, with the precision of a professional smoother of waters, shortened the ceremony and released us from the podium. As I descended the steps I felt a quick hindquarter tug and saw that Harry was wrapping my disgrace in a small plastic bag and depositing it in a nearby garbage receptacle.

And so we muddle on, elevated one minute, dragged down the next, relying on one another for comfort (and an opposable thumb). Harry gave me a pat and said that he was proud of me. Zest said that the event had made great television. As the crowd drifted away for mid-morning snacks, Harry, Ivan, Zest, and Tabasco discussed what was to come next. Santorini had planned another meeting in the theater during which he promised to unmask the murderer; Zest had apparently convinced him to allow part of it to be a séance conducted by Ivan Manners. This should have been welcome news, but I could not concentrate.

I began to pace.

As I've pointed out, most dogs are compulsives, and under great stress those compulsions can grow worse. I had never thought myself compulsive. Even the anxiety of previous adventures had not evoked compulsions. But here I was zigzagging around the deck tracing a small space as if my life depended on it. I scratched at one corner of the imagined space and collapsed in a heap. Without realizing it, I had re-created the dimensions of our cozy apartment back in Manhattan. I may have thought I was up to the task of venturing out into the wide world, but the limits of my Labrador nature seemed to be closing in around me. I should have been listening to the next moves of the group and plotting my own, but instead all I heard was the shrill whine of my own anxiety.

During the worst of the storm I had seen a woman sitting with her husband in the lobby of one of the dining rooms. She had been hysterical, nearly out of breath, and repeating the same thing: "We're going to sink. We're doomed." No matter what her husband said, she was convinced of this. Threats—invisible to everyone else—were all around her.

From our first moments aboard ship I had been uncharacteristically anxious, but now the strain had broken me. I stood up and began to trace out the walls of our apartment once again, racing around and around. Where was Imogen? I would never see her again or restore our home or live to get off this damn ship and back onto dry land. I saw Kitty's dead face in my mind. The dagger in her back. Our ransacked stateroom—ransacked by whom? Heard Blinko's grave warnings. Saw the bland menace of Frank Booker lurking about. I ran around and around tracing the room, tracing the room, and if I could have spoken I would have sounded exactly like the hysterical woman.

"What are you doing, Randolph?" Harry asked from what sounded very far away.

"Isn't that cute? I think he's going crazy," Zest said.

SOON EVERYBODY RECOG-
nized that my behavior was, in fact, not
cute.

Tabasco directed his Muttering at me to no effect.
Then I felt Harry's arms wrap around me. He stopped
my running. I tried to pull away but he held me.

At first he was stern. "Randolph," he shouted.
"Stop."

But when he saw that didn't work and realized that
I was shaking badly, Harry became very gentle.

"It's going to be okay," he said, and for an instant I
knew that he understood and it felt like we were back
home again sharing a pizza or take-out spareribs and
watching television before our evening walk in Central
Park. He repeated this prediction of an imminent
"okay," and it began to calm me.

But then Melody Buttermold did something completely unnecessary.

"These'll perk him right up," she said and before
Harry could intervene or my normal willpower protect

me, the cruise director had placed two morsels right under my nose. I gobbled them down.

It was Sedadog Extra™ *The Snack That Calms as It Thins*.

Harry was angry. Miss Buttermold was unrepentant. Yours Truly was stoned.

"Everyone's on medication these days," she said. "It's perfectly safe."

Except for the stray spillage of beer in my water bowl (as happened once during one of Imogen and Harry's parties in our carefree days), I had never experimented with mood-altering substances (the toxic encounter with a chocolate-glazed doughnut at the United Nations an exception). I was not prepared for Sedadog Extra™.

Time began to warp again, but this time it was free from anxiety. The humans around me seemed to become caricatures. Harry continued to express his displeasure with Miss Buttermold's decision to "drug my dog" and Zest and her crew, trained to get all angry emotions on camera, actively filmed the dispute. Tabasco held forth on his philosophical problems with dog mood-altering drugs.

None of this mattered to the subject of the dispute, who began to notice how beautiful all the colors were and how very funny. And speaking of funny, the deck chairs were funny, noses were funny, the Scandinavians cleaning up the mess left by the "canine triathlon" were funny. Since I had no ability to laugh, all of this hilarity was channeled into my tail, which cranked up to propeller speed. I heard Miss Buttermold remark on it in support of her pro-dog-medication position.

"See how happy he is," she insisted.

But I wasn't happy at all. I had merely been relieved of my senses. Of course, no dog drug researcher could actually know the intangible effects of the medication on the subject, since a dog couldn't communicate the experience. Harry and the others moved on to their next destination, and I gladly followed them. I might have seemed "cured," but I now had as much free will as an iron shaving drawn to a magnet. I was still as troubled as before, but now I wasn't causing any trouble for my humans. I also noticed that my olfactories seemed confused. Tabasco had switched scent with Harry. A potted palm we passed smelled like Imogen. A door smelled like lasagna.

Nor could I pay attention to much of what was being said. Our group passed through the corridors discussing the events of the previous night. Tabasco had disappeared. Zest said she was planning on interviewing people and wanted Harry and Ivan to join her. Santorini, the self-appointed ship's detective, was mentioned, as was Captain Bostitch (for "you know, nautical color"); half a dozen members of the audience could give their accounts of what had happened in the moments before the covers were lifted off the cages and Kitty Tabasco appeared murdered. But when this was supposed to happen I did not catch because the

wallpaper had begun to dance. By the time this performance had finished, Ivan was talking about wiring
Tabasco into a paranormal antenna, Harry was nodding
vigorously as if this were one of the breakthrough concepts of the last hundred years, and Zest was insisting
on filming it. Drug-addled though I was, it was impossible not to sense Zest once again reaching amorous
tendrils out toward my owner. As we climbed a flight of
stairs, the ship leaned ever so slightly and Zest clamped
onto Harry's shoulder to support herself. Her hand lingered there. Had I not been distracted by the lilacs
growing out of Ivan's head, I would have taken some action. But I didn't need to. The strange-looking Scandinavian appeared from behind us on the stairs and
pushed between Zest and Harry.

"That's not very nice," Zest complained to the
sailor's back. But the sailor, who smelled like Imogen
but with that crisp standard-issue cologne overlay, did
not stop or turn around.

Sedadog Extra™ affected me in waves. One moment I seemed to be surfacing back to my old self and
the next I was submerged again in a world of hallucina-
tion and pleasant whimsy. None of the urgent and important work that my gray matter needed to do was
possible in my current state. Fortunately, my companions seemed intent on taking a break. Perhaps it was
the fact that less than a day was left before we disem-
barked in Curaçao and the pleasure aspects of the

cruise had been shortened by the tropical storm. Whatever the reason I welcomed it.

Music was playing nearby. I gathered that it was real
because everyone else seemed to hear it. Soon we found
ourselves in Key West Cove, a backwater open-air
lounge decorated with papier-mâché palms and fake
thatch huts. Our neighbors from the bowels of the
ship, the college coeds and alcohol pioneers, were here
colonizing oblivion with a fifth pitcher of sangria. I
slumped beneath the table while above me my humans
ordered drinks. The server put a bowl of water next to
my head with a little paper umbrella in it.

The band was singing the anthem of the beach culture, a song that concerned the singer's search for a lost
saltshaker, his unpromising present, uncertain future,
obsession with a certain frozen alcoholic concoction,
and satisfaction with a recently obtained tattoo from
Mexico. My head began to sway to the melody. The
singer noticed and decided to change the words.

"We're just wasting away in Dogarittaville...," he
sang. The sun warmed my paws. Drinks arrived above
and there was laughter. A xylophone joined the singer
and the band played and played. I rolled over onto my
back and watched the clouds pass far above us, shape
and reshape themselves against the deep blue of the
upper atmosphere. Such infinite variety and such lack
of purpose. I drowsed.

Some time later my eyes opened. I was still on my
back. Someone had put a straw hat over my head and

draped a lei across my chest. I rolled over, stood up, and shook. The drug seemed to be wearing off. I no longer saw things that weren't there or thought inanimate objects had personalities and wanted to be my friends. Harry, Ivan, and Zest had restricted themselves to one drink each and were still earnestly discussing what and how they were going to film. I tasted the Sedadog™ nuggets in my mouth. I knew that if I encountered these psychotropic tidbits again I would have trouble resisting—the gravy flavor was delicious, and the drug-induced mental holiday for my overworked and melancholic mind was appealing.

Chairs were shifting, the trio were getting to their feet, and I began to listen to the conversation going on above my head.

"So the so-called detective guy's going to do his Agatha Christie reveal and then we're going to do the séance or vice versa?" Ivan continued.

"Not sure," Zest said.

"I don't want the séance being used as window dressing," Ivan said.

"Trust me," Zest said. "My work isn't superficial."

Less than fifteen minutes later Harry and I were in Jackson's suite. Jackson and Marlin were not alone. Ms. Hadley Purcell, the pet portraitist, and Cha Cha, her estimable Yorkie, sat on one of the couches. Ms. Purcell was showing Jackson her etchings.

"Harry," Jackson said. "Ms. Purcell has just bailed me out of the brig. You missed the action. I nearly brained that lout from Stanford with my sword-cane. He had the impudence to say that my thesis on Rubens's espionage work smacked of conspiracy theory grist and the very worst kind of B-movie tripe. When the man from U Chicago decided to join his side, I knew that action must be taken."

"Academics at arms, call the militia. Me? Under the table at this point," Ms. Purcell offered.

"Laugh if you like. The academic is the last savage," Jackson said.

"Chicago boy puts his mug down with a decisive thud; our friend here draws a sword. Next stop Alcatraz."

"I'm in her custody," Jackson said.

"I love your mosaics, but I don't have anything clever to say about them," Ms. Purcell told my owner.

"Thank you," Harry said and then motioned at Ms. Purcell's etchings. "Those are very good."

"These little things? I'm only a hobbyist," Ms. Purcell said.

"I disagree," Jackson said.

"Bigger things happening aboard ship than etchings and academic swordplay," Ms. Purcell said. "Lady with a dagger in her back."

With that introduction, Harry updated the two on Kitty's second death and related matters. I decided to wander over to Marlin whose potted palm, because it was a pleasant day, had been placed on the balcony. The

Guatemalan tree sloth seemed calmer than he had on his first day. A Guatemalan tree sloth is by far one of the most intelligent animals I have met. It is still a mystery to me why I understand Marlin, however, since he delivers his potent brain work in solid bursts of sound that take me minutes to decipher. I've described his communication as akin to the shrill bursts of a fax machine—dense with meaning and coming at intervals. There is never a need to repeat a question for Marlin, only the patience to wait for the answer. When the answer arrives it will be worth it.

Marlin had already picked up most of the Tabasco story from listening to his owner speak with Ms. Purcell. What bothered him was not the how of Kitty Tabasco's death in a cage—this he felt assured could be determined if Yours Truly climbed into the hidden compartment himself to determine the mechanisms involved. To quote Holmes, Marlin said, once you had eliminated the impossible, whatever remained no matter how improbable must be the truth. Kitty did not stab herself. The placement of the dagger square in the middle of her back ruled that out. Kitty was not dead before she got into the secret compartment in the cage. The stagehands had seen her climb into it. Milton Tabasco had not done it, because he was never near enough to do it.

Marlin concluded, as I had, that it must be some kind of mechanical trick and that somehow the cage

was rigged to deliver the fatal dagger thrust. He believed that I should not doubt my sense of smell:
Milton Tabasco was the guilty party, if not directly
responsible then the architect of his wife's death. I
had smelled a murderer. Now the question was catch-
ing him.

But Marlin—unlike me—had not only lingered on
the cage or ways of tying Milton to it. What bothered
Marlin was what had happened to Kitty on the first
night. Marlin was more attuned to the nuances of the
classic murder mystery, having watched untold hours of
Agatha Christie remakes with Jackson at his home at
the Belvedere. Most sophisticated murders, Marlin
pointed out, used the same kind of smoke-and-mirror
deceptions common to the magic trick. The magician
only has a moment to distract, but it is during that moment that the trick is made possible. No trick happens
at the instant it is perceived to have happened; it happens at some other moment.

Why, Marlin continued, if Kitty was "scheduled" to
die during the magic trick, would she have been made
to die twice? Certainly a distraught or jealous spouse
"jumping" off the back of the liner in the middle of the
night was preferable to a death in a cage in front of an
audience. One of the ways a magician distracts is by
physical flourishes: the wave of the hand, flutter of a
handkerchief, brief flash of empty pockets, or punch
line of a joke. Kitty Tabasco on the Poop Deck was the
distraction. Her jealous departure from dinner was too

obvious and too memorable. It was meant to be noted by the diners. As Marlin spoke I remembered what our friend Detective Davis had said during my adventures at the United Nations about Imogen's behavior in the boardinghouse—how she had caused people to remember her actions by being rude to them. Negative emotion, threats, angry voices, fear…these things stick with us.

Marlin concluded: Kitty Tabasco on the Poop Deck was a setup. At this point I reminded the Guatemalan tree sloth that Kitty's scent had been genuine when I had spotted her on deck after the scene in the dining room. Even as I said this, I already recognized the flaw: Actors tap genuine emotions—painful memories—to make themselves cry. This could be one explanation. Alternatively, Kitty could simply have been upset, but that didn't detract from the reality of this planned distraction.

Then Marlin supported his point further: Dinner had finished at nine thirty. Harry and I had walked the deck shortly thereafter. So sometime between nine thirty and ten PM, we had seen Kitty. An hour after this, another passenger and her dog had seen Kitty in the same spot. And still later, some time around four AM, Kitty had presumably leaped from the boat, causing a passenger now known to me as Vicki LaBoom to belatedly sound the alarm and stop the ship. This was further evidence that Kitty wanted to be seen in the hours prior to her supposed jump from the ship. And she wanted to be seen crying.

"Why?" I asked.

After a several-minute pause, Marlin blasted back.

"She was distracting everyone's attention from something else."

"From what?" I asked.

But Marlin had no answer for me. He reached out slowly for a frond, brought it to his mouth, and began to chew. The rest of the truth would be left to my own limited devices to reveal.

I was about to return to my owner across the room when Cha Cha interrupted me. The terrier with the gingham bow and the air of urban sophistication had ignored me during the visit. The life of other dogs is a great unknown to Yours Truly. For the most part, as I've indicated, I find their communication fragmented and baffling. Where other dogs babble, I sing. I have met some exceptions, but rarely. I expected a similar disappointment from this owner-described New Yorkie no matter how in control of her facial expressions she seemed to be. I was wrong.

Cha Cha, all six and a half pounds of her, could certainly put a sentence together.

"The problem you have will only be resolved with hard facts," Cha Cha said. "Facts that can be leveraged, exploited, deployed, and masticated."

"Masticated?"

"Chewed over."

"I know what *masticated* means," I said with a touch more hauteur than necessary.

"Fabulously smart, are we? Going to mark our intellectual territory, are we? Typical male," Cha Cha said. "What matters here isn't the battle of the big brains. It is using those big brains in a practical way to get to the bottom of things, isn't it? That's what you want, don't you?"

"Yes," I said.

"Not acting that way for most of this trip, have you," Cha Cha demanded. "Rolling in here half drugged. Disgraceful. Couldn't resist the old psychotropics, could you? Going psycho in the tropics, are we? I saw you with the sombrero on the head, lolling on your back, swaying to the music, paws in the air—don't think I didn't."

"Miss Buttermold crammed them down my throat."

"Don't tell me you didn't enjoy it, belly boy. Beef Stroganoff? Chicken Kiev? Cajun Shrimp?"

"They were tasty," I admitted.

"People dropping like flies and you're high as a kite," Cha Cha continued. "I've heard better things about you from Jackson Temple over there—he's been talking my mistress's ear off. Not that she seems to mind. A West Sider and an East Sider together at last. Really they're meant for each other—please forgive the putrid sentiment."

"Forgiven."

"So let's get to work."

"Us?"

"Of course. People are dying."

"Only one person at this point."

"So sure about that?"

I thought a moment and realized that I was not so sure about that. Something Marlin had said had begun to sink in, grow roots, and sprout hazy mental leaves. If Kitty on the Poop Deck was a distraction, what was she a distraction for?

As if she were reading my mind, Cha Cha expressed my conclusion for me. "A distraction from something similar going on..."

"And by similar, you mean someone or something falling over the side of the ship," I continued.

"Exactly."

"But why?"

"Because..." Here Cha Cha was momentarily stumped.

"Because there's no better way of getting rid of a body than by disposing of it in the middle of the ocean in the middle of the night, but doing so aboard a ship with fifteen hundred passengers, many of whom might be expected to be roaming the decks and the corridors at all hours of the night, is risky and calls for a place-holder."

"Placeholder," Cha Cha said. "I like that. Very elegant. Very apropos."

"Kitty Tabasco was the placeholder," I said. "That's why she hung around and was meant to be seen hanging around the same spot. That's why she made a scene at dinner. And that's why she disappeared for a few days and everyone was made to think that she was the one who went overboard. If you wanted to commit the perfect murder, the untraceable murder, you would need to plan on being seen in the act even if you weren't in the end."

"Because someone staring out a porthole or stuffing their face at a buffet might just happen to see a body falling past at four in the morning."

"And there would have to be a ready explanation that would cover the bases."

"But what happens when Kitty Tabasco turns up two days later and everyone is supposed to believe that no one went overboard. What then?"

Cha Cha had a point, but all of my cumulative literary and living experience managed to produce a useful answer.

"It's the mystery of memory and time."

"Profound."

"You've heard the expression *the moment has passed*," I asked.

"Of course I have," Cha Cha said, shaking her head with subtle exasperation and making the gingham bow quiver.

"By the time Kitty appears again—dead as it were— the moment of that first night has already been put to rest in any accidental witness's mind. It's the quintessence of the magician's method again. It's the nature of narrative, the telling of a story. As long as you get readers, audience members, witnesses to move forward quickly enough, they will not bother to retrace their mental steps or raise questions even when contradictory facts are introduced. In other words, Kitty's return dead or alive two days later is logically inconsistent with what they saw on the first night—someone going overboard—but by this point if any questions are raised in their minds, which I doubt, they will be dismissed because the memory will have faded. The moment has passed."

"I like," Cha Cha said. "So who went overboard and why?"

My 2.3 pounds of smoothly functioning gray matter had gained momentum and my thoughts were leaping ahead, surprising me with my own conclusions. The fragments of our shipboard journey were coming together.

"I have a theory," I said. "And it would be a great help if you could assist me in testing it."

FIFTEEN MINUTES LATER Cha Cha and I were approaching room 2301, a modest triple-bed, two-room cabin, on Deck 12. This was the monks' quarters. Cha Cha, with that skewering wit so often seen in city types, had correctly condemned me for being too slow to chase down the truth of the mystery. The storm had hampered me, of course, as had the latent canine compulsivities that had become so apparent. But now these would be battled back. Santorini's gathering and the séance, which was only two hours away, was the moment that a conclusion could be made and justice served—but much would have to happen before then. I had little faith in Santorini, the hotel detective, identifying the full cast of the guilty—he was intent on "nailing" Tabasco—but if we reached Curaçao before the guilty were identified and apprehended, they never would be.

Part of this conviction came from my last snout swipe of Tabasco's seat the night before. It had taken the better part of the day to realize fully what it told me. Tabasco was guilty of something but deeply remorseful and, more important, genuinely surprised by Kitty's death. Things had not gone as he had anticipated. He could not be the murderer of his wife. But Cha Cha's mission had to do with another death.

"I'm going to scratch on the door," I said. "And when the door opens, you will race into the room. Go everywhere and inhale deeply."

"I don't have the nose that you do," Cha Cha said. "It's been ruined by years of exposure to the perfume spritzers in Bloomingdale's."

"That's fine," I said. "If it's all the same to you, I can sniff you."

"Forward," she said. "And humiliating. As if I'm a swab."

"That's exactly the way you should think about it," I said in my eagerness, not recognizing my insensitivity. "Go everywhere in the cabin. Jump on the beds. Go under the beds. If there are any rugs be sure to roll on them. Don't forget to—"

"I've got the picture, fella," Cha Cha said.

I scratched on the door.

Nothing happened.

I scratched again.

Feet approached.

"Yes?" a voice asked. I recognized it as belonging to the thin monk, Brother Phillipus of Antioch also known as Gary.

I scratched again.

"Yes?"

Cha Cha whined and delivered a sharp yap yap.

"Hide behind me," I instructed.

"Yes, my liege," Cha Cha said.

The door opened a crack. Brother Gary poked his head into the hallway, looking both ways and then down at me.

"Go," Brother Gary commanded.

At this point, as per our hastily conceived plan, Cha Cha raced from behind me and through the narrow opening where the thin monk stood.

"What?" the monk exclaimed. To my surprise and alarm, he shut the door in my face. Immediately I feared—irrationally I suppose—for Cha Cha's well-being. All I could hear through the solid metal door was her barking and whining and what I imagined was a vaudevillian chase through the cabin as Gary tried to catch the six-pound New Yorkie. A table toppled. Someone fell heavily over a chair. There was colorful language. More barking. Then it all stopped.

I felt a sudden iciness grip me and told myself this was foolish since there was no real danger. To Gary we were only dogs doing doggie things, not investigators gathering evidence. But still I had my doubts about the monk's goodness and Cha Cha was, after all, such a tiny thing in a very large and hostile world.

The commotion started up again behind the closed door. There was a grunt and another yap. I was angry with myself for sending Cha Cha into such a situation. Finally the door opened and the monk emerged looking disheveled and holding Cha Cha aloft by her collar. He dropped her into the corridor and slammed the door.

"Are you all right?" I asked.

"Lovely," Cha Cha said.

"I should have gone in."

"You never would have fit through the door."

I waited for Cha Cha to recover—she was clearly ruffled, and her gingham bow was askew—but despite appearances, the New Yorkie was ready to debrief.

"Nothing special," she reported. "I jumped and rolled on everything, but if you were hoping that I'd see something out of the ordinary, I'm sorry to disappoint you."

"Did you see both rooms?" I asked. I knew the rough layout of the cabin, having seen a map of each deck over the course of the week.

"Everything."

"Who was there?"

"Just that guy."

"No one else?"

"There was a weird smell," Cha Cha said. "I can't describe it. Oh, wait, yes I can. It was like that waft of air you get standing at the top of the subway stairs."

"Rats and things that live underground."

"Exactly."

"May I?" I asked, preparing Cha Cha for a snout sample.

"Keep it above the neck."

Cha Cha was quite a wit.

I quickly snuffled the top of her head, an area the size of a doorknob. The snout sample confirmed what I had suspected.

Despite her perfume-impaired olfactories, Cha Cha had given an apt description of the room's smell. The scent that covered her coat and obviously dominated the monks' quarters was close to that found in a New York City subway station, but there was an added dimension: sudden, messy, murderous death (of course this, too, was always a possibility in a New York subway). I had regrettably smelled this particular brew several times in the previous year. Upon finding Beatrice, the con artist, dead beneath the double-folio-sized Audubon bird book in an Upper East Side library, Michael slumped and bleeding at Iris's dining table, and later the corpses of the angry poet, Abraham Pollop, and the recyclable lady in the boardinghouse. Too much death, but the exposure had taught me to recognize death's signature qualities instantly.

Someone had died suddenly and homicidally in the monks' cabin. The scent was faint enough that I knew that the death had been some days earlier, but strong enough to confirm that it had been after our embarkation on the present journey.

"And you'd be interested to know there was blood

on the floor—on the carpet right in the middle of the floor—but they'd moved the table as if to conceal it, which was obvious because it looked ridiculous where it was and got in the way of everything," Cha Cha said.

"Blood," I said. "And that was the table that fell over?"

"He was very nervous about me being there."

"It's understandable," I said. "That's the reason they aren't letting the Scandinavians clean."

"And the Scandinavians aren't happy."

"No," I said. "They are not, and the monks have no doubt had to stay on guard against the bucket brigade. Because there are two things that they do not want to have to explain: First, why there is a bloodstain on their carpet, and second—"

But I was interrupted before I could finish. The door to the monks' cabin opened and Gary emerged. He glared at Cha Cha and Yours Truly, closed the door behind him, double-locked it, hung a DO NOT DISTURB — PRAYER ZONE sign on the handle, and stalked off down the corridor.

"There's no time," I said.

A few moments later we were on the stage of the theater. All the principals were present. We had arrived just after Gary. Harry, Ivan, and Zest were already there, and Zest was doing a mike check with her crew. Apparently, the séance would come after Santorini's revelatory presentation of the facts as he saw them and his fingering out of the suspect. The cage in which Kitty

had died stood in the middle of the stage, luridly illuminated by a single spotlight. Beside it was a long table
covered with a black tablecloth—candles down the
middle—and lined with chairs. I wondered how
Santorini had managed to secure everyone's coopera-
tion in this effort if it meant the potential unmasking of
one of them as a murderer, but my question was answered by Zest, who was speaking to her production
assistant–cameraman.

"Now, you've made sure that everyone has signed a
release?" she asked.

"Everyone's done it," the assistant said. "No one
wants to miss out."

"Even Bostitch?" Zest whispered.

The captain, looking particularly annoyed, had just
arrived.

"We've got him covered under the corporate cruise
ship release," the assistant noted. "Legally he's a performer. Anything he does on ship can be filmed by us
and used any way we want."

"Perfect."

I left Cha Cha near Harry and Ivan, who were setting up a handful of ectoplasmic sensors around the
perimeter of the stage, and sauntered over to examine
the cage. As per Santorini's instructions, nothing had
been touched. Or at least it seemed that way from the
front, but at the back I found that a panel hung open on
hinges. This was the opening to the compartment into
which Kitty Tabasco had secreted herself prior to her

death. It was only a short hop off the floor, and as I stood beside it, the smells wafting down to my nose were profound and intriguing. I suspected that the device was somehow responsible for Kitty's death, but I had no idea how. I wished that I could get a better scent and a closer look at how the device worked.

Cha Cha's words returned to mind like a sharp rebuke. Was I really lazy? Even worse, did I lack courage? Was I not ready to take action and put myself on the line to get to the bottom of things? Here was an opportunity to settle these doubts.

I jumped up into the compartment, but my hindquarters hung in the air behind me. The opening was tighter than I had thought and I was stuck. I imagined Jock Johnson barking in my ear about my weight and despite myself felt a cascade of canine shame (so easy to conjure up).

"Oh my," Cha Cha said from somewhere outside the cage. "Not too sensible."

I sucked in my generous belly and with one giant effort managed to pull myself forward until all of me was inside.

Two things became immediately clear: First, Kitty Tabasco would have been lying on her back with her head in the direction of the hatch (I was lying on my stomach and felt handles pressing into my lower back), and second, this particular exploration had been a bad idea (someone closed the hatch behind me and then I heard Santorini's voice instructing the cage to be spun the way it had been on the night of Kitty's death).

As the cage spun I decided to dampen my developing panic by searching out scent clues. Kitty Tabasco had shed several distinct emotions in the seconds before her death: excitement of the showgirl-popping-out-of-the-birthday-cake-to-surprise-everyone variety followed by a sudden burst of excruciating pain and terror and then something I had not anticipated. I smelled regret, as if Kitty Tabasco knew that she had made a serious mistake. This last part, I assumed, reflected the moment of her death. I did not have too long to reflect, however, since with each spin of the cage I felt a blunt object pushing farther and farther into my soft belly. Had I been positioned in the opposite direction and right-side up, as Kitty had been, this blunt object would have been pushing into the middle of my back.

The cage spun a third time and then began a fourth rotation. With the motion I heard a mechanical ratcheting sound that seemed to correspond to the motion of the blunt object. Even with my acute hearing, I had not heard this on the night of the show beneath the crowd and the general racket of the performance. By the time the cage had finished its fourth rotation, the blunt object was pushing so hard into my belly that I thought I might lose an organ. I swore off all future midnight buffets. My girth was hateful to me now that death loomed. Why had I been so busy with other things, so distracted in my life? I should have read more, experienced more, focused more on that which was important. Some lines from Emily Dickinson came to mind: *I could not stop for Death, so he kindly stopped for me* ... The pain grew fiercer. But just when I could take no more, the cage stopped spinning and with the sound of a coil being sprung, I found myself being shoved upward and shot out of the compartment and onto the floor of the cage.

Gaping mouths surrounded me. My belly throbbed from the recent abuse. My brain, however, teemed with a triumphant conclusion.

"Randolph," Harry said.

"Aha," Santorini exclaimed in a dramatic, inquisitorial fashion. "The dog has revealed the mechanism of the crime."

"If you mean the rotational ratcheting spring-flipper that moves the participant from the hidden compartment into the viewable area of the cage so that the trick can actually work, you're right. That's the mechanism," Tabasco snapped. "I designed it. I even patented it. United States Government Patent Number IJ205312."

"Well done, Mr. Tabasco," Santorini said. "You have just convicted yourself of the murder of your wife."

"What are you talking about?"

"That device killed your wife."

"Don't you think I know that?"

A few of the assembled gasped. Santorini's confidence was shaken.

"You do?"

"Of course I do," Tabasco said. "How else could she have been killed? It's obvious that someone tampered with the mechanism."

"How?"

"By putting a dagger in the prod," Tabasco said. "The mechanism alone couldn't hurt a fly. Look at the dog. He's fine."

I wasn't fine although I was now on my feet. And despite my recent trauma, I was scampering around the cage trying to jog off the effects of the trick.

"He's not fine and neither were the other dogs you used in your experiments as you developed this device."

Santorini held up a piece of paper. "I found this information on the Internet," he said triumphantly. "It is a citation from the International Association of Magicians and Illusionists for the suspicion of mistreatment of animals in your magic acts. The citation outlines the charges—which you never contested. They include building devices that could potentially harm 'animal surrogates.' It goes on to say that you used dogs as 'guinea pigs' to test magical devices that could compel performers to behave a certain way in the unveiling of a trick by applying 'coercive physical stimuli.' "

My belly still ached from the "coercive physical stimuli."

"Old news," Tabasco said. "Because of that I got out of the magician racket, and the rest is dog-training history. I was wrong. I admitted it. I moved on. That's the

American way. Second, third, and fourth chances. That's why we have liberal bankruptcy laws and such, so if you mess it up royally, you get a do-over. I went a little overboard with the animals in my magic acts. I'm not proud of what I did, but it taught me how to empathize with our fellow creatures. But if you think I killed my wife with this thing, you're just plain wrong. I'm not stupid and I'm not obvious. Anyone who wanted to kill her and knew that device could have jerry-rigged it with a knife. And it could have been done at any time. God knows the cage wasn't guarded. We loaded it on in New York and it's been sitting backstage ever since. Could've been anybody. Even you."

Santorini looked down at the floor. It was clear he had already run out of ammunition.

"Is that so?" he asked.

"Afraid it is," Tabasco said. "Now, do you think you could go and find whoever really killed my wife?"

Santorini was about to say something when a woman's voice boomed toward us from the entrance to the theater.

"Mickey, baby," the woman screamed. "You better not be playing detective again. You promised me shuffleboard and margaritas at four."

"Playing detective, sir," Captain Bostitch demanded.

Santorini, if that was his real name, turned red.

"For God's sake, Helen, can't you keep your mouth shut. I'm coming already," he shouted.

Zest gestured for her cameraman to do a close-up on the faux hotel detective's face.

"Do you mean to say you're not a real detective," Zest asked.

"That's right," Santorini said. "But I *was* on to something."

"Not even a hotel detective?"

"Mickey," the woman at the top of the aisle boomed again. "Getta move on, will ya?"

"I've really got to go," Santorini said. "I didn't mean any harm, I just have a thing for mysteries—reading them mostly—I'm an accountant in my day job. It's a recurring problem, I guess. I'm in treatment, but I couldn't resist this one."

"Self-control, sir," Captain Bostitch advised. "Self-control."

After the would-be detective abandoned the stage, Harry released me. The truth about the detective threatened to dissolve our group, but Zest—intent on getting something more on film—managed to rally everyone to stay. The television celebrities, Milton Tabasco and the two monks, agreed readily, but Zest had to apply a great deal of charm to the captain, who deemed the prospect of a supernatural intervention "balderdash."

"Your opinion is totally valid, Captain," Zest said. "But we need your natural charm and authority at the table to make this work."

She patted the captain's epaulettes and he, too, took his place at the table.

Everyone was assembled, the lights were dimmed, and a certain spookiness set in, heightened by the odd vibrato voice that Ivan Manners employed from his place at the end of the table.

Ivan informed all gathered that he would be attempting to contact Kitty Tabasco's spirit in an effort to learn what had happened to her. Before this, however, he was going to have Mr. Apples fly around the table as a kind of preliminary psychic measure.

"Birds are highly attuned to the spirit world," Ivan pronounced. Harry looked on gravely.

As usual it pained me to see adults—especially one who was entrusted with keeping me alive—succumbing to such irrationality, but the behavior also offered an opportunity to plan my next move. The fact was that I already knew who killed Kitty Tabasco.

It was Kitty Tabasco herself. The residual scents in the hidden compartment and Milton Tabasco's own had confirmed it. Kitty would have known how the device operated and how to make it lethal. But at that moment proving the suicide of Kitty was less important than preventing those guilty of the actual murder aboard the *Nordic Bliss* from disembarking the ship in Curaçao.

This would require rapid action and a great deal of luck. I hurried from the theater just as Ivan released Mr. Apples and the rainbow lorikeet began to hop from person to person. Cha Cha followed at my heels (or, more accurately, kept abreast of me as I moved at top speed through the corridors).

"What's the hurry?" Cha Cha asked.

"I need a keyboard and a printer," I said as we took the first flight of stairs.

We reached the library a few minutes later. Cha Cha distracted the librarian by hopping onto her desk and allowing herself to be scratched under the chin and then, in a maneuver worthy of those phony movie dogs, picked up the librarian's purse, jumped off the desk, and ran out the door. The librarian ran after her. I was left alone to snout-type and print my message.

There was no time to waste. I yanked the paper from the printer and headed back to the theater. When I arrived, Ivan had just begun a spirit-summoning incantation. Milton Tabasco tried to look bored. Gary, the thin monk, tried to look disinterested. Vicki LaBoom tried not to look at Milton Tabasco, but she could not help herself. She was completely infatuated with the Dog Mutterer. Vicki LaBoom—as much as it pained me—was the weak link and my target now.

There was enough room between the substantial LaBoom and her neighbor, Zest, for me to slip in unnoticed and deposit my paper on the table in front of the singer.

"What's this?" Vicki LaBoom asked aloud. She reached for one of the candles and illuminated what I had written.

"You little bastard," she muttered after she had read it. "No way are you gonna pin it on my darling Miltie."

Ivan stopped speaking. Everyone looked at LaBoom. LaBoom got to her feet and leaned over the table at Gary.

"You did it," she said. "And everybody's gonna know about it. We only gave you an itty-bitty hand."

The "it" in question was the murder that *had* taken place, the murder that Kitty Tabasco had distracted from and the murder that Cha Cha had supplied the evidence for. This murder involved greed and ambition. The seeds of this murder might have been planted long before the *Nordic Bliss* left her berth in New York, but Harry, Jackson, and I had been the ignorant witnesses to its first conspiratorial planning session. That occurred when Gary and Milton Tabasco had met in the early hours of the cruise and hatched the plan that would lead to a body being thrown overboard that night. They weren't arguing about ratings, as Jackson had supposed; they were hammering out a plan to eliminate the greatest impediment to an even greater dog-training business: Brother Timothy Sextus, the fat monk.

The fat monk had resisted. In fact, he had been resisting for months. He had already tried to scale back the schnapps production on the grounds that it had gotten out of hand and violated their religious mission statement. Now he believed that the dog empire must be shrunk, possibly even eliminated lest his brothers go too far astray. This I had gathered from my reading of news stories about the competition between the Dog Mutterer and the *Dog Is God Spelled Backward* bunch. In the calculus of Tabasco and Gary, Brother Timothy had to die and so he did, killed by his two brother monks in their cabin before the *Nordic Bliss* had even reached the Atlantic. This same calculus also demanded that everyone have dirty hands. That was why Kitty Tabasco was on deck for several hours drawing attention to herself and why Vicki LaBoom reported seeing her jump and why, I assumed, Milton Tabasco had helped the monks carry the body on deck and dump it overboard in the wee hours.

There was one last part to this murder plot, and if left uninterrupted by Yours Truly it would have meant that the crime would have remained undetected. It was the part that Vicki LaBoom was going to play in exiting the ship. The fact was that a passenger can't simply disappear mid-transit without eventually being missed. To disembark, all passengers must be accounted for. The fat monk's absence would have been noticed in Curaçao . . . if it weren't for Vicki LaBoom. A performer on the ship and a native of the island, Miss LaBoom could count on slipping off the ship unremarked. This meant that she could double as the monk, hood firmly covering her features as he was shuffled off the ship and made to vanish forever.

Had I voice, I would have outlined all of the above for the people sitting around the table. But all I could do was set the ball in motion and hope that the anxiety and strained loyalties would lead to sufficient revelations. They did.

"What are you talking about?" Gary said.

"You know what I'm talking about," Vicki LaBoom said. "I'm talking about you being all ready to blame Miltie for what you did to your friend. How you killed him."

"Killed who?" Zest asked.

"The other one of them, that's who," Vicki said. "They killed him. Miltie only helped cover it up a little. So don't believe what he told you already. What I just said is the truth."

"Vicki, baby, what are you doing?" Milton Tabasco demanded.

"Miltie, that guy ratted you out," she said. "It says so right here."

She held up the piece of paper.

"You idiot," Gary said. "I did no such thing. Can't you see you were set up?"

With that Gary ran out of the theater.

"What's going on here?" Captain Bostitch asked.

"I think we just witnessed a confession to a crime we didn't even know happened," Zest summed up.

Milton Tabasco stood. Ivan, motivated perhaps by some vision of man-of-action heroism, grabbed him by the shoulders.

"No you don't," Ivan said.

"Yes I do," Tabasco said and pushed Ivan over his chair. Then he, too, ran out of the theater.

"Are you getting all of this?" Zest asked her cameraman. But her cameraman had run out of batteries.

I gave chase with Cha Cha in tow. We raced up the aisle and down the long corridor that led to a staircase and the aft of the ship. Tabasco was well ahead of me and pushing his way through passersby, one of whom was Jock Johnson, Pet Wellness Officer.

Johnson flashed me a thumbs-up as I sped past.

"Keep up the good work," he encouraged. "You'll be fighting fit in no time."

We raced on, up one flight of stairs, down another corridor, and up a second flight. Tabasco ran through a lecture hall where Dame Norma Aqualung, a writer of what the critics called absurdist mysteries, was chastising an audience member who had criticized her works for lacking realism.

"Is life realistic?" retorted Dame Aqualung. "For one of your so-called realistic novels—let alone a realistic mystery—to work, you need five thousand suspensions of disbelief, three thousand outrageous coincidences, and one thousand deus ex machinas. Mind you, no reader or reviewer will ever notice these offenses against the laws of nature and probability, but if you put in one fanciful twist or one slightly unbelievable name—like my own, for example—suddenly everyone's pulling their metaphysical hair out. Who are we to say anything about reality? That dog there could be more philosophical than you. Realism, my eye ..."

Dame Aqualung leaned against the wall at the front of the room to permit Tabasco, Cha Cha, and Yours Truly to race by. "If you could kindly take this matter outside," Dame Aqualung requested, and so we did. Another long corridor and several more flights of stairs both up and down until a poetic circuit was somehow closed and the chase finally came to an end. We were out in the open air and Milton Tabasco was pressed against the far railing of the Poop Deck. The ship was slowly turning, and off the starboard side the distant outlines of an island were visible. We had finally reached Curaçao.

"This is a load of crap," Tabasco said. "I've worked hard for everything I got."

Tabasco began firing his Tourette's syndrome communication technique at me. But I growled to blot out the sound and neutralized it. Earlier I had observed a small dog who was constantly yapping appear completely immune to the Mutterer and realized that creating a wall of sound against his compelling language could serve as a defense. Seeing that he could no longer command me, Tabasco addressed me directly in plain English.

"You and I could go far," he said. "You figured out all of it yourself, didn't you? I've had my eye on you. We could make oodles of cash together."

I explained that I wasn't interested in oodles of cash and found murder abhorrent.

"He had it coming," Tabasco said.

"No one has it coming," I said.

Then Tabasco began to cry, and despite my wiser sensibilities, the programmed part of my Labrador's brain that prompts me to support the humans in my vicinity commanded me to draw near to him. But as soon as I was close, Tabasco scooped me up and with a grunt threw me overboard.

DOG IN THE WATER

———————

CRAB CAKES ON THE BEACH

I HAVE NOTED BEFORE THAT time is relative and seems to open up for all of the sensations and experiences that it needs to fit. This happened as I fell the preposterously long way from the Poop Deck to the water. As I fell, I had ample time to confirm my hypothesis on why Tabasco and the others needed a cover story for the disposal of the monk. There must have been a hundred portholes passed on the way down, but even more moving—for as I fell, I sensed a kind of elegiac sadness and self-pity creeping in—was the glimpse of the buffet tables through the broad plate glass of one of the dining rooms. And as sometimes happens in moments of shock, a particular detail stood out. In this case it was the center tray heaped with *pigs in a blanket*. Many would enjoy those delectables, alas not me. I fell on. I continued toward the propeller-roiled water beneath me, reflecting on how ironic it was that I was once again falling off a ship into the water. Time seemed to slow. It was such a long way down. Then just as I reached the sea, I was aware of someone falling beside me. I expected to see Tabasco making a break for the mainland, but instead I saw the strange-looking Scandinavian waiter whom I had encountered on and off since we'd left New York.

We hit the water at the same time and with tremendous force that seemed to crush my rib cage and drive all the air out of my lungs with a single powerful gust. The water was warm and frothy and it took a very long time to claw my way back to the surface. When I finally did, I bobbed about still stinging from the impact but in one piece. The *Nordic Bliss* receded, steaming on to its momentary dockage in Curaçao. There would be no helicopter rescue as there had been in New York Harbor. No one aboard had sounded the alarm, but then I watched as another body plummeted off the ship and into the water. Three in the water now.

I looked around for the Scandinavian waiter. Just as I had paddled myself in a full circle, he breached the surface ten feet away. But he was no longer a he. He was a she. And she was Imogen.

I would have assumed that I had died in the fall and was now floating in some liquid corner of paradise had it not been for my stomach rumbling with hunger and a chest that was beginning to throb with pain.

Imogen's mustache hung off her lip like a slug. The waiter's hair had vanished and in its place were my mistress's dark honey locks, still pinned down to her scalp to accommodate a wig.

"Randolph," she said and swam over to me. "Randolph."

Imogen was my true owner. Imogen had picked my puppy self out and up from among the wood shavings, the indignities, and the loneliness of the pet shop and made me her own. Now, despite myself, I began to back away from her in the water. I did not mean it. Or at least the better angels of my nature did not mean it, but there was a resentment deep within, a reservoir of pain and remembered agony that would not easily dissipate. Why had she abandoned us? Even if she had been in great danger and was still in great danger, both Harry and I would have eagerly shared it with her just to have her near.

Imogen moved a few feet closer to me. I cringed and back-paddled. Despite the ruins of her disguise, she looked very nearly the same as when she had left us a year and a half earlier. Though, at the corner of her eyes she seemed older, as if she had been frowning for too long and the emotion had stuck.

"Randolph," she said. "Don't you remember me?"

Had I the vocal cords, I would have shouted an unqualified and uncomplicated *yes*. But my Labrador's body needed a moment to rid itself of an acute sense of betrayal and hurt. It seemed as if once again I was seeing, smelling, living through the months after her disappearance: the long winter days as Harry and I unraveled into toxic bachelorhood, words from the books I read during that time returned with a painful heaviness of their associations with her absence, the mixed messages about her fate, and most of all the way that time can be a painful mockery, seem like a shell of itself, when the one you love is no longer present in it. To endure we build a kind of false peace, an incomplete structure to keep off the heavy weather, but to live fully again this structure must be disassembled and abandoned.

I had once read an account by Konrad Lorenz, the famed animal behaviorist, about a reunion with a dog that he had left in a zoo and how the dog was initially cold to Lorenz upon meeting again. But then the dog in wolf-like imitation had thrown up its head, howled, and run toward him in frantic greeting. I'm not an expressive type beyond the instinctual excesses, but if this could clear the air I would give it a try.

I delivered a lupine howl and then for added measure a full-body shake. Imogen smiled and it was like opening a window that had long been shut. Harry, not Imogen, was the communicative one in our family. Imogen had always preferred to nod, whistle, or snap her fingers rather than address her canine charge with superfluous words. And now was no different.

"There we go," Imogen said as she reached me. She cupped my head in her palms for a moment and looked me straight in the eyes. She didn't speak aloud, but she managed with this gesture to express the following to me: "You've done such a good job and you've been very brave."

Then she gave me a quick pat on my head, turned, and began to swim toward land.

"Come on, beautiful," she called to me. I paddled after her.

A few minutes later, there was a shout. I had assumed that whoever had fallen or jumped off the back of the *Nordic Bliss* had swum off in another direction. I was wrong. It was Harry.

"Harry," Imogen said, stopping for a moment to turn in his direction. "Why are you here?"

"Where else would I be?"

"My love," Imogen said. "I'm sorry. I'm so sorry."

"What were you thinking?"

"About you," she said. "Always about you."

"It didn't seem that way."

Harry had, like me, probably expected himself to be warm to her and instead found himself momentarily cold. There was at bottom the simple, inescapable fact that our mistress had left us alone with no explanation for such a very long time. Harry pushed himself onto his back and spouted a mouthful of water into the air as if he were playing in a swimming pool and not far from land in waters possibly shark-infested.

"You look all right," Harry said.

"You look lovely," Imogen said.

"You look lovely, too," he said.

"You don't have to say that."

"I mean it," Harry said. "Lovely."

"We'd better get going," Imogen said. Harry had swum close to her, almost within reaching distance, but she swam away from him. "It's going to get dark at some point."

So we swam for a while in silence and when I got tired, which I did long before either of them, Harry and Imogen got beside me and sidestroking together buoyed me up and moved us forward. We made steady progress like this, and the shoreline grew more and more detailed. When we were about a quarter of a mile away, we stopped for a break.

"We're lucky," Imogen said. "Do you see that beach?"

Harry nodded.

"That's the beach that I always told you about," she said. "The one beneath the stars."

"The stars that you drew on the boardinghouse ceiling as a clue for us?" Harry asked.

"Took you a while to figure that one out," she chided.

"I think I did pretty well considering you didn't leave too much to go on," Harry said. His tone had been warming, but at this exchange it grew a little colder. "Why aren't you here already?" he asked. "Wasn't that the point of the clue? To get us to come all the way down here and find you on the beach?"

"You found me, didn't you?" Imogen said and began to swim again.

"Did we?" Harry asked. "It's more like you found us."

"What does it matter? We found each other," Imogen said. "Come. Aim for the far corner of the beach. There's a little beach-grill-and-kayak-rental place there. You'll love it."

Half an hour later we emerged from the light surf on a white sand beach empty except for a flock of birds picking at crabs and a young man dragging a kayak to the water's edge.

"You fall off that cruise?" the young man asked.

Harry and Imogen nodded but did not speak. They didn't seem to have the energy for it. I was utterly exhausted and had done only a small amount of swimming.

"I was coming to get you," the young man said. "Guess I won't have to now."

"Things are slow to get started down here," Imogen whispered to Harry and then said to the man, "Thanks anyway."

"No problem," he said. "I've never seen anyone jump off one of those things before."

"We couldn't wait to get here," Imogen said. "Can we order drinks?"

"Sure."

"And that crab cake sandwich you're famous for," Imogen said. "I had it once. Can we get two?"

"Make it four," Harry said and then, looking down at me, changed his order again. "Five."

"And the fries," Imogen said. "Double order please."

"And a few beers," Harry said.

They arranged for a water bowl for me and borrowed dry clothes for themselves from the young man. I don't know how the shack stayed in business, but finding solitude and good service together in one place was very pleasant.

Soon the food arrived. Instead of sitting at the tables near the shack, we took the food back closer to the water and sat down on the sand.

"Delicious," Harry said, eating half a crab cake sandwich in one bite.

"Isn't this place great," Imogen said. "And it's such a beautiful time of day."

The sun was setting somewhere behind us. The last of the light had turned the water a brilliant green and hinted the far horizon with a pale orange and purple.

"There's a lot that I want to know," Harry said.

"There's a lot that I want to tell you," Imogen replied. She covered his hand with hers and gave a gentle squeeze. "But what you need to know right now is that I'm here."

"That's not enough," Harry said. "I don't care what danger you're in or who's after you or why they're after you, I never want you to go away again."

"I won't."

"You can't," Harry continued as if he hadn't heard

her reply. "I'm not going to let you. It doesn't matter what can happen to me. I don't need to be protected."

"I'm not going anywhere except with you," Imogen said.

"You promise?"

"I promise."

There was a long silence and several long sips of beer.

"Why did you ever leave?" Harry asked.

"You folks good?" the young man interrupted. "I'm closing up for the night."

We were "good" and he disappeared. I had the sudden canine instinct to chase a bird down the beach, but I resisted. My animal spirits—so long dampened by Imogen's absence—were returning to me.

Imogen told of the months after discovering the true identity of her mother, Iris, the run from her and the multinational spies intent on stealing her uranium fortune, of playing competitors against each other, of the death of her childhood friend in the boarding-house. Most important, Imogen finally explained why she had let Harry believe she had died over a year and a half before.

"You've got to understand what happened that night I first went away. I was going to return."

"With your bread."

"With *our* bread." Imogen smiled a soft, bittersweet smile. "But when I was approaching our apartment I saw two men outside on the street. Overton had warned me that if Iris didn't get me, there were plenty of people who would. I watched the men for a while and I knew Overton was right. Those men were there for me and there was only one way to protect us. I had to make everyone believe I was truly gone and that meant making you believe I was gone, too. I had considered doing it before I left the apartment that night, but those two men decided things."

"Cymbeline," Harry said, echoing the encrypted clue that Imogen had left in her journal for us.

"I counted on you taking a while to figure that one out. I'm so sorry, Harry. I watched you whenever I could. I thought about you always. But you know that."

Harry stared at Imogen for a long time before he spoke.

"Even after I knew you were alive I never really considered how hard things must have been for you. You're some girl, Imogen."

They were both silent for a while.

"Well, tonight we have nothing to worry about," Imogen finally said.

"And tomorrow, if we have anything to worry about, we'll worry about it together," Harry said.

"I'm not going anywhere," Imogen said.

Yours Truly found a place a healthy distance from the pair and fell asleep with the sound of waves and the knowledge that a certain order had been restored to our universe.

"Randolph," Harry called from the darkness. "Knock yourself out."

Something flew threw the air and landed in the sand between my outstretched paws. It was a crab cake and I ate with gusto.